The

OFFERING

a novel

DESIRÉE BOMBENON

LIVE OAK
BOOK COMPANY

Published by Live Oak Book Company
Austin, TX
www.liveoakbookcompany.com

Distributed by Live Oak Book Company

For ordering information or special discounts for bulk purchases, please contact Live Oak Book Company at PO Box 91869, Austin, TX 78709, 512.891.6100.

Design and composition by Greenleaf Book Group LLC
Cover design by Greenleaf Book Group LLC

Publisher's Cataloging-In-Publication Data
(Prepared by The Donohue Group, Inc.)

Bombenon, Desirée.
    The offering : a novel / Desirée Bombenon. -- 1st ed.

    p. ; cm.

    Issued also as an ebook.
    ISBN: 978-1-936909-54-4

    1. Family vacations--Hawaii--Fiction. 2. Children of divorced parents--United States--Fiction. 3. Voodooism--Hawaii--Fiction. 4. Rescues--Hawaii--Fiction. 5. Hawaii--Fiction. 6. Suspense fiction, American. I. Title.

PS3602.O62 O44 2012
813/.6   2012936025

First Edition

For my family and X forum, your support means everything,

For Janine and Joel, you are the smile in my heart, and

For Marc, I love you—always.

CHAPTER 1

IT WAS A GOOD DAY TO BE ALIVE. Sitting out on the lanai, Amanda watched the waves roll in with graceful arcs, reaching their peaks and then crashing down into a swirl of white froth over the rocks like giant beer foam. She sat and watched wave after wave for hours. Amanda and Jake celebrated the New Year in quiet retrospection.

They had a wonderful relationship. It was built on trust and respect, with a little intrigue intertwined. They met while Amanda was doing a practicum for her degree in business administration. She was bent on working for a company that was on the cutting edge of technology. Back then cellular mobile phones were the rage and still are today, for that matter. Amanda was so keen on the technology she was invited to join the team full-time once she completed her degree. Working for the wireless company, Amanda quickly found herself immersed in a rapidly growing business and was promoted on a regular basis. Jake and Amanda ran into each other quite often around the office, and it wasn't long before he asked her out for a business lunch, which quickly became a regular occurrence. Initially the lunch chatter was mostly about work, the people, the products, and the future of the company. Soon they were discussing other, more personal subjects, such as the geopolitical situation around the world and their thoughts on the environment and religion. They found that they really had quite a bit in common, at least with their opinions on such matters. Jake found out that

Amanda had had a very difficult childhood, that she felt people could only count on themselves to create the spirituality that is so needed to help us through difficult situations. Jake had conceded his dislike for any religious order, simply due to the corruption and harm that has come about throughout history from institutionalizing religion and using it for selfish reasons and not necessarily to help people. He too felt that spirituality was best kept in your own mind and soul. Although Jake and Amanda felt it was important to have a belief, it was just as easy to create that from within, although they hesitated to give it a name or call it a religion. The two of them became best friends first and then eventually were married. Their children were scattered on different continents: one in Germany while he finished a program in graphic design and photography at the University of Cologne, and the other working up in Canada at one of Jake and Amanda's many companies. So it was easy to take a break at their second home, a quaint little condo at the Beach Villas Resort in Ko Olina on Oahu, Hawaii; they toasted in the new decade and said good bye to 2011.

It was not like back in 2000, when there was pressure to bring in the next thousand years with hoopla and grandeur; the human race had survived to see Y2K. There was far less excitement or anxiety now, more than ten years after the twin towers fell. Regimes all over the world were crumbling. While the Occupy Wall Street movement was targeting America's elite, Libya was celebrating the death of Gaddafi; the world was in flux.

There was something heavy in the air. Amanda felt it was akin to a storm brewing in the distance. All the crazies were coming out of the woodwork, hanging their hat on a word or phrase from some biblical or ancient transcript that was misinterpreted or translated incorrectly. They were claiming 2012 to be the year of the apocalypse, the end of the world, the final meeting of good and evil in an ultimate fight to triumph over what would be left of civilization. Amanda was a believer in one world and the idea that everyone was an equal citizen. *It's really like* Star Trek, she thought. *Here we are all one race—the human race—with that one overarching prime directive: don't interfere with another species' culture or way of life. But what if we are all the same species and by not interfering withhold intelligence that could help people in other communities? Then are we truly being citizens of the world? Yes*, Amanda thought, *and now you sound like those Americans who think the world can only be safe if we impose our thoughts and beliefs on everyone else. The world police, big brother, is watching over you, and if we are all the same, then we can all be right. This is a crazy world*, Amanda mused.

Watching the joggers going by on the path below, she smiled and observed: some were toned, looking comfortable on their run, and others were overweight and determined to make a change in their appearance and form life-changing habits for the New Year.

This was the normal scene for the first day of the New Year—everything was "kosher," as Jake would say. Amanda's analytical mind worked at the picture, and she still felt an ominous chill, even with the weather at a comfortable 72 degrees so early in the morning. Her female instincts were kicking in for no apparent reason.

Amanda turned to Jake, who was busy browsing away on his computer next to her, and asked, "Something feel odd to you about this New Year's Day?"

His eyebrow went up. "Yeah, we're in Hawaii?" he said with a smirk. "What do you mean, 'something feel odd'?"

"Oh, I don't know, like heaviness?" Jake didn't take his eyes off the screen, just uttered a no in her direction. She left it at that, which was unusual for Amanda because most days she would prattle on about her gift. Jake had never quite bought into her clairvoyance. He called it luck or educated guessing in most instances; it was his way of dealing with it. But sometimes Amanda would say something that, sure enough, would foretell what would happen at some point in the day. Those instances were disconcerting to Jake.

This was Amanda's gift, or curse. Amanda had been very young, too young to remember exactly, when she first started getting the strange feelings that felt like a tummy ache to her at the time. She noticed that she would see a scene in her mind or in a dream during a nap, and before she knew it, it was happening in reality. When she first learned of her special instincts, she would try to stop people from boarding an airplane or crossing the street if she felt anxious. She would wake up in the middle of the night and call the police. More times than not, it ended up with her in trouble and then all kinds of questions and detainment when something did go wrong. She learned to keep her mouth shut. Nobody believed it anyway.

Several times that gut feeling that we all have, and most of us ignore, had saved her butt. There was the time she was about to board a train in Moscow to go to Saint Petersburg to meet Jake while attending a Young Presidents' event. She could still picture it clearly. It was November 27, 2009. Amanda reached the platform for the Nevsky Express but at the last minute felt her stomach churning with anxiety. By this time she had learned to trust her gut instinct and decided not to board and instead to rent a car and drive the 440 miles. That night, a bomb exploded, the train derailed, and twenty-six people were killed, with many more injured. It was a tragic occurrence that involved the misguided reasoning of unreasonable terrorists. Her feelings of guilt over not having said anything to anyone prior to the disaster were something that she would have to live with for the rest of her life.

Jake thought the Nevsky train incident was pretty good instinct on her part. For some reason Amanda found herself in stranger situations than most people. Although Jake trusted Amanda's gift, he bought a large insurance policy on Amanda the next day. She took it as a compliment. She knew she was a valuable strategic advisor to him and their group of companies, but he had just upped her worth in case something were to happen. Jake also had a hefty insurance policy to ensure that the companies were looked after, not only for their children, but also for all their employees and the foundation that Jake and Amanda had formed a few years earlier. They followed the mantra "Without sacrifice there is no success." They started with nothing and grew it into a very comfortable empire, which included giving to numerous charities. Many worthy causes around the world depended on them.

Jake had started his business during the new age of cell phones and mobile units. Its head office was located in Calgary, Alberta, Canada. However, they considered themselves a global entity with affiliates such as Jakanda Enterprises, a well-known, privately held company based in Bermuda that had a variety of portfolios, including land development, wholesale distribution, and a major interest in the oil sands exploration happening in Northern Alberta. Jake also had an interest in flying. Soon after the success of his wireless enterprise, he got his pilot's license. Achieving this quickly, he expanded his qualifications to flying jet planes and helicopters. The Bell JetRangers were his favorite. He was the closest thing to a bird without wings. Amanda worked on building their business process–outsourcing company, which quickly grew to providing services globally. The rapid growth of the businesses came with lots of headaches, including finding the right talent, keeping good workers, and balancing the needs of customers with the goals of the companies. This made for challenging and uncertain times. It was not without true grit and determination that they survived, especially with the recent economic crisis. Add to that some smart investments in real estate, oil, and gas at the right time and, voilà, lots of work and lots of success. As they developed their businesses, they became noted for their philanthropic endeavors and community work.

Of course, the hard work took its toll. Amanda was very involved in helping Jake build their empire until a health scare caused them to reevaluate their lives. They were potentially at their peak in business growth when, during a regular checkup, Amanda's doctor found a lump in her left armpit. After several tests determined that it was cancer, Amanda began treatment. It was caught in the early stages and, with a combination of surgery and treatment, she was now clean. Though successful, the treatments left a permanent emotional scar on both Jake and Amanda. They both agreed that their time together would be better spent enjoying life and not engulfed in work. Jake read *The 4-Hour Workweek,* which gave him the push he needed to wean himself off his BlackBerry, which had become an appendage sometime during the previous five years. Finding the right people to run the companies, including their daughter, they were able to take an early retirement, acting only in leadership and advisory roles.

"Amanda, are you having a premonition?" Jake's voice bellowed clearly from the bedroom of the condo.

Amanda stirred. *When did he ever get up and leave the precious computer?* she thought. "No," she echoed back, "no prems right now. Why?"

"Oh, I thought you would get a *feeling* that my coffee was now cold and needed a top up."

Very funny, Amanda thought, and got up to make him a fresh cup. Just then Michael Jackson's "Bad" started playing loudly. It was Amanda's ringtone. She loved it! It was a shame Michael had had to go the way he did. He was one of her idols growing up. She remembered dressing up in the skinny pants and the red leather jacket. She desperately begged her mom to buy her the white glove when she was twelve. Amanda and her friends would spend hours break-dancing, trying to reproduce the dance moves by Michael in his *Thriller* video. Michael Jackson, she felt, was probably deep down a very disturbed but good person. The fact that his doctor was found guilty of involuntary manslaughter didn't make her feel any less pissed off that the pop idol was dead. She looked at the caller ID. *Hmmm, wonder what Bernie Wright wants*, Amanda thought.

Bernie was a local Royal Canadian Mounted Police officer whom Amanda and Jake got to know back home. He had a place next to theirs in the Shuswap Lake Estates in British Columbia. They became close right after his wife ran off with his partner. He never saw it coming, and he frequently came over to drown his sorrows in a good mojito made with fresh mint grown right there on the mountainside. Shuswap Lake stretches out in four large arms with over nine hundred miles of shoreline. It is one of the most pristine and beautiful areas of the Okanogan. From the long May weekend to Labor Day, it is a summer-long reckless party place, houseboats dotting the lakes and shoreline, with music blaring and fireworks shooting off all night long. But in the early spring and late fall, the lake is calm and the air is still warm. You can lie out on the dock at night and enjoy the brilliant starlight and moonlight reflecting off the dark lake. It is heaven on earth, a spot Jake and Amanda refused to give up. Bernie too refused to give up the cottage on the lake when he and Gail broke up; Amanda didn't blame him.

Bernie and Gail had one daughter together and shared their time with her just about fifty-fifty, which wasn't typical. Most often, the father either doesn't want the time or the mother refuses to share equally when it comes to custody. It was unusual for Bernie to call except during the summer months.

"Hey Bernie, happy New Year!"

"Hi Amanda, happy New Year to you as well. Sorry to disturb you guys. I know you're in Hawaii, but . . . well," he stumbled, "I have a favor to ask you."

"You're not calling so we can pick up some chocolate-covered macadamia nuts, are you? By the way, the drink of the day is the Mai Tai out here."

"No, nothing like that, Amanda. Listen, this is important."

She heard the concern and tension in his voice and immediately felt a ping in her gut. It was just a small one, and it was mostly due to the slight tremor in his words. "I'm listening."

"Amanda, last week I had my daughter for Christmas. It was my turn. Gail had her for New Year's. You know how we alternate every year. They left on the twenty-ninth to go to the Big Island in Hawaii, but they never checked in to the hotel. Gail promised she would allow Taylor to call me at midnight your time in Hawaii, which is 3:00 a.m. here. When she didn't call, I tried Gail's cell phone, and it's either turned off or the battery is dead. It went straight to voice mail, so I left a message but haven't heard back. I called the hotel this morning, and that's when I found out they never checked in. Amanda, you know Gail and I have a really great understanding of how important our relationship with Taylor is. We never screw up on stuff like this. I am really worried."

"Did Keith go with them?" Amanda hated bringing up Bernie's ex-partner. She never did like Keith. She remembered the night when Bernie invited Keith to a charity event for teenagers who were addicted to drugs and/or alcohol, and Keith decided to tie one on. He blurted out to a group of friends that the kids couldn't hold a candle to the amount of booze he drank when he was a kid, and now he's a cop. "Kids these days are too pampered. Let me have 'em for a week. I'll straighten 'em out." Amanda was sufficiently embarrassed. Later that evening Keith also pinched Amanda's butt as she was heading to the ladies' room. What a jerk! When he moved in on Gail she disliked him even more.

"Yeah, he did. I tried his cell and same thing. I already called Air Canada and confirmed that they did land and get off the plane. They also got their luggage, or someone did, but the hotel claims they never checked in. I also tried texting Taylor direct on her cell phone. Taylor's phone is restricted from long distance, but it allows texts, so I sent her a couple but haven't heard anything. She is a text addict, so I am not sure what could be going on."

"Did you call the authorities?"

"I did, and they are opening up an investigation. They asked me if maybe they changed their mind about which island they wanted to stay at. I told them that was unlikely, but they are checking it out anyway. They are working with local teams on each of the islands to see if they can track or trace any transportation to the other islands. I don't know, Amanda, Taylor would have insisted on calling me. She was very excited about getting to stay up. She thinks fifteen is pretty much adult enough to have champagne and toast in the New Year. When she was younger, Gail and I always had a pre–New Year's toast 'cause we felt she was too young to wait up until midnight, and 90 percent of the time she was fast asleep way before anyway. I am really worried that something is not right here."

Is this why I had the feeling of heaviness earlier? Amanda wondered. She couldn't quite distinguish it yet, so she didn't let on to Bernie. It would only make him worry more. "Listen, Bern, Jake and I will take a quick hop over there. Who's in charge?"

"Detective Tao," he answered.

"OK, got it. Detective Tao on the Big Island. We'll go from there, and I will keep you informed. Keep your cell phone charged."

"Amanda, I am so sorry to interrupt your time out there with Jake, but I know you have great instincts, to put it mildly. You helped solve those two cases that everyone else had given up on; you were able to come up with answers. I know you don't think it's any big deal, but you know it's a gift, right?"

Yeah, or a curse, she thought. "No problem, Bernie. We'll find them. Everything will be OK. I'll give you a call from the Big Island." Amanda clicked off and went to let Jake know that they were off on another adventure.

Yikes! She knew the look she was going to get. She quickly made his fresh cup of coffee and sauntered into the room, ready for the lecture.

"What!? It's New Year's Day, for crying out loud. How are we gonna get over to the Big Island and start a search-and-rescue mission?" Jake was not pleased.

"Umm, I don't think disappearances are in any way coordinated to avoid the holidays, love. And how do we get over to the Big Island? Well, you *do* fly planes, and you *do* have an American Express Black Card," Amanda said with a grin. Jake gave her the look, the same one he always did when he was unsure about what she was up to. She called it his "Spock look," because one of his eyebrows went up and the other went down simultaneously. And although it was quite funny, she knew that Jake meant business when he did it. He then went to get his pilot's license. He knew a couple of the guys who rented aircraft on the island personally, since he and Amanda often went to visit friends in Kauai and Maui during the holidays, so he made a call and, even on New Year's Day, managed to secure a plane.

They prepared for the trip. *Who knows where this will take us?*, Jake thought. He packed all kinds of climbing gear, some first-aid items, and a few devices on special loan to them. Jake was well connected in the technical world, and he was often called upon to test out the latest innovations from some of the leaders in design engineering. He often was allowed to hang on to these items, and because they now spent the majority of their time at the condo in Oahu, this was where most of the gadgets were stored. This wouldn't be the first time Jake and Amanda had decided to involve themselves in something that could prove to be dangerous, so he packed both of their handguns and some ammunition. *Just in case*, Jake thought.

CHAPTER 2

THE ISLANDS WERE BEAUTIFUL AT THIRTY-FIVE HUNDRED FEET. They chartered a twin-engine Piper Navajo. It had eight seats, including the cockpit. Amanda informed Jake that they would be bringing back Gail, Taylor, and Keith with them, so they needed the room. Jake loved her confidence, but he was not so sure.

"Why are we flying so low?" Amanda asked.

"So we can actually enjoy some of our vacation," Jake said as he pointed toward a small pod of whales with a calf breaching the surface in graceful, slow arcs. *Wow!* Amanda thought, *this kind of sighting is so amazing.* Hawaii was one of three places in the world the humpback whales migrated from Alaska's cold waters. Starting in early fall, it took them approximately four to six weeks to make the long journey. You just couldn't beat Hawaii's natural beauty and simple pleasures, whether it was whale watching or relaxing on a quiet stretch of the beach with a good book.

Amanda knew they were on an urgent mission, yet she couldn't help enjoying flying over the water, floating just above the clear blue sea with the sun in their faces. They skimmed by the towering walls on the north side of Molokai and up past the island of Maui, where Jake and Amanda had once rented a plane and flown to have dinner and drinks, staying overnight at the beautiful Westin Maui. When they got to the Big Island, Jake advised the local control tower that they would be doing a slow tour and informed them of altitude and route prior to landing. The control tower acknowledged and assigned them a new transponder code. They flew right over the Kilauea volcano. Seeing an actual active volcano at any angle was impressive, and being right above it was absolutely amazing. Jake was careful to stay out of the thermals coming up from the volcano, but the hairs on the back of Amanda's neck went up regardless. Despite coming to the islands for twenty years, they had never been to the Big Island before, and Amanda did not realize how large it was, or how lush and green. It was understandable why so many tourists had begun to spend their vacation at the Big Island over the more popular islands of Maui and Kauai. Jake and Amanda had always preferred the hustle of Oahu and Waikiki Beach. They had spent many evenings eating at Chuck's Steak House at the Outrigger Waikiki, with the music drifting up from Duke's and the sun setting on the most popular beach on the planet. Now seeing the Big Island for the first time, Amanda could see herself spending some time hiking and exploring this amazing mass of land.

Caught up in the moment, Amanda nearly forgot their mission. "OK, big boy, remember why we're here? Land this thing." Jake nodded, but she could see the disappointment in his eyes as he radioed the control tower that they would be starting their descent inbound and asked them for clearance to approach Kona International Airport. Kona International was smaller than Hilo, the main airport, but it was on the nicer side of the island, according to Jake. He had used his Visa Black Card concierge service to book a room at the Outrigger Royal Sea Cliff near the airport. It had luxury accommodations on top. "After all, we are on holiday," he reminded Amanda. Jake was kind of Bondish when it came to his adventures outside the office. His thinking was, if they had to go on a mission, it was just as easy to do it in style. Amanda couldn't agree more.

As they were coming in for the landing, Amanda thought about how the Big Island continued to grow in size due to the lava trails flowing into the sea—very interesting. The island's name was actually Hawaii. However, in order not to cause confusion with the state, which was also called Hawaii and consisted of all the islands, the big island was known as Hawaii's Big Island. She remembered reading about how you could enter several ecoregions on this one island—from the desert-like conditions on the southeastern shores to the snow-capped mountains in the north, which brought skiers and snowboard fanatics alike. The island boasted the world's tallest peak; Mauna Kea stood over thirty-three thousand feet, measured from the ocean's floor. The lush wet rain forests were another wonder found in the windward lowlands. Amanda had heard many people speak about Waipio Valley, or the Valley of the Kings, and wondered if she and Jake might have time to explore it on this trip. The island was also surrounded by beautiful beaches, and not with just the regular white sand but also black and green sandy shores. She was looking forward to seeing them. Kamehameha the Great, who unified the Hawaiian Islands during the time of his rule, was born and raised on the Big Island. She felt excited about this trip, except for a slow rising feeling in the pit of her stomach, the one that gave her the proverbial red flag that should have had her asking Jake to file a flight plan directly back to Oahu that very minute.

CHAPTER 3

"OK, TELL ME AGAIN EXACTLY WHAT BERNIE SAID." Jake's eyebrows were at their peak as he exaggerated the word "exactly." *It's funny how his eyebrows go up at the ends, giving him a devilish look*, Amanda mused. It was funny most times, unless Jake was pissed off. Then it could be somewhat disconcerting.

"I told you everything. There really isn't much. They left on the twenty-ninth. They were supposed to check in that evening at the Castle Hilo hotel in the main city, but they didn't show. Their luggage was removed from the belt—whether by them or someone else, nobody knows. Jake, it's best we meet with Detective Tao; he may be able to help us with what they have put together so far."

"OK, you're right, Amanda. I just don't want to spend the first week of 2012 on a wild goose chase. What if they decided to take a cruise of the islands—you know, rent a boat or something? Keith is a sailor, you know."

"Yep, Keith is a lot of things," Amanda said ruefully

"Hey, none of that talk. Gail made her choice; be nice." Jake smiled, but he knew as well as she did that Keith was a bit of a con artist and often claimed many great talents in which he was not quite as competent as he suggested. The problem was that Keith really believed he was great, and it often got him in trouble. Amanda couldn't help thinking of the time they were visiting Bernie and Gail for a Saturday afternoon barbecue and Keith showed up just in time for dinner, as usual. Bernie was having problems getting the fire lit because there was a pretty nice summer breeze blowing. Jake watched as Bernie struggled and moved to help him when Keith put his hand on Jake's shoulder and said, "I've got this, big guy. You take a seat with the ladies here." Jake waved him through. All three of them watched silently as Keith moved over next to Bernie. They couldn't hear what was being said over the breeze, but they could see Bernie shaking his head and Keith then walking off and coming back a few minutes later with a can of some sort of liquid. Amanda remembered thinking, *This doesn't look good.* Next thing there was a loud swoosh sound and the entire barbecue pit looked like it was on fire. Bernie had jumped back, but Keith was slower and had singed his hair, eyebrows, and most of the hair on both his arms. Amanda inadvertently giggled out loud at this memory and then jumped at the sound of a man's voice on the phone.

"Detective Tao. How can I help you?"

"Hi, Detective. Amanda Bannon here. I believe . . . "

"Oh, yes, Ms. Bannon," the detective cut in, "I have been expecting your call. Your friend Bernie Wright mentioned you would be calling, and he mentioned your *special ability* as well."

Oh great, Amanda thought, *another skeptic.* Not that she wasn't used to that tone, but it often made things far more difficult when it came to getting cooperation in an investigation.

"Yes, Detective Tao, I understand you may not necessarily feel I can be of any assistance. However, I think if you can keep an open mind over the next few days, if nothing else I *do* have personal knowledge of the missing individuals that may at least be helpful in your investigation."

"Yes, I guess that could potentially be of some value, Ms. Bannon. However, I strongly recommend that you leave it at that and do not interfere with an open investigation. Doing so could get you in a tremendous amount of trouble . . . trouble that your RCMP officer friend cannot help you get out of, if you know what I mean?"

Amanda could hear the tinge of irritation mixed with something more menacing in the detective's voice. Again, she had that anxious feeling in her stomach. *Oh, stop overreacting,* she told herself and then blurted out, "Thank you, Detective. We will make every effort to stay out of your way. You have my cell phone number if you need anything from me, or if you want to call the hotel, we are staying at the—"

"Outrigger Royal Sea Cliff," the detective said, cutting her off. "Yes, I know."

Amanda grimaced but kept her voice clear and steady. "Yes, that's correct, Detective. By the way, would you mind letting me know if anyone saw any of the missing individuals—Keith, Gail, or Taylor—at the luggage carousel in the airport?"

"Not that it would make much of a difference, Ms. Bannon, but, yes, there was a family who was sitting next to them on the plane."

"Oh, and what did they say, Detective?"

"Ms. Bannon, I am not sure that relaying this information to you will be of any help."

"Yes, I understand that is what you may think. However, there could be something they told you about how the family was behaving that would seem strange to someone who knows them well."

The detective fell silent for a moment, then sighed. "They told us that they saw the three of them grab their luggage. The man, Keith, even boasted because their luggage had come off so quickly. He laughed as he went out the door, taunting the other family because they had to wait for their holiday to begin. Needless to say, he didn't leave a very good impression."

Well, that sounded right, especially the part about Keith. "Anything else they noticed?"

"That's the last anyone can remember of them."

"What about the taxi or car services?"

The detective fell silent again. After a few seconds Amanda spoke softly: "Detective, please, I know you think this is a waste of time, and I can't say anything that is going to change how you feel right now, but it really isn't going to hurt to let me know."

"The taxi steward said he did not have a group fitting their description that he could remember, so they must have had alternate transportation. We checked the rental agencies. No rentals to Keith Stevens or Gail Wright, or Gail Stevens, for that matter.

"Now, is there anything else I can do for you, Ms. Bannon? I do have a very serious investigation to attend to." The detective's sarcasm was thick.

Amanda simply said, "No, thank you." She pressed the end button on her cell phone while it was still pressed to her ear and then said, "Yeah, fuck you too, Detective." Jake's eyes were wide with shock as she pulled the phone away. Amanda smiled and said, "Oh, I ended the call before I said that out loud, but it still felt good."

Jake's Spock eyebrow went up again, and then he grinned. "Come on, we have some lost people to find, and I'm hungry. I need food!"

Amanda's stomach began to growl. She remembered that they hadn't eaten since a bagel and coffee on the lanai. So much had happened since breakfast. It was almost 4:00 p.m. They had missed lunch completely. "Well, we can't investigate on an empty stomach. How about a kalua pork sandwich and a cold Longboard Island Lager?" The traditional Hawaiian sandwich, a longtime favorite of Jake's, was named after the traditional Hawaiian cooking method, first used in the early 1900s. The pig was salted and rubbed with herbs and wrapped in banana leaves. Finally, it was buried in a pit with hot stones, where it would slow cook for a few hours. These days, there were several aboveground methods that had been developed with artificial mesquite or liquid smoke to mimic the old-school flavor. To Jake it didn't matter—kalua pork sandwiches couldn't be topped.

"Sounds about right." Jake almost drooled the words out as he thought about the sandwich and the local beer. "I don't think I will be flying again today, so I can get away with a couple of Longboards."

CHAPTER 4

"OK, LET'S GO THROUGH THIS AGAIN." Jake motioned with his kalua pork sandwich and, through a mouthful, continued. "Three people get on a plane to the Big Island; three people get off. They get their luggage, but they don't get a taxi or a rental car. Someone else had to be there to pick them up. There was no struggle, because people would have seen that. It was someone they knew or a company they hired in advance. I could see that smug-ass Keith hiring a car for them on Gail's credit card, paid by Bernie, couldn't you?"

Amanda looked at Jake, barbecue sauce smeared all over the side of his mouth, with a bit on his nose. *Boy, I really love this guy*, she thought. "Honey, I can't take you seriously with pork sauce smeared on the end of your nose." Jake quickly wiped at the sauce with his napkin and continued.

"Yeah, but, Amanda, think about it. They were picked up by someone they felt OK about getting in a car with, right? I mean, they were in a busy public place. If they felt threatened, it would have showed; people would have noticed. Did the detective check the rental-car and limo companies?"

"Jake, he probably did, but you are right about one thing. If Keith did hire a car, he wouldn't have paid for it. He's too cheap, and Gail would've just taken a cab. I can't see it. There is a piece missing here, and I think I will give Bernie a call. Just talking to him could trigger some tiny bit of info that might give me a clue. Jake, the other thing that concerns me is that their flight came in at 6:30 p.m. on the twenty-ninth. It's been three days."

"Well, one thing is for sure." Jake seemed to have lost his appetite as he put the juicy sandwich down. "If it's something really bad, we probably are already too late. I am not saying that they aren't alive. I am just saying that the chances of this turning out to be a happy ending goes down by 10 percent with each day that goes by, and after ten days, I can tell you chances are nearly zero for a good recovery."

"OK, babe, I get it. So that gives us seven days or less. Let's get to it." Amanda downed the rest of her beer and threw some bills on the table. Jake held the door as she jumped into the Viper they had rented for the trip around the island. Jake always rented the best sports car available, just in case.

"You wanna drive, Amanda?" Jake asked.

"Nope, go for it. I need to call Bernie, and you corner in high gear better than I do."

Jake grinned. He loved it when she talked carspeak.

"Bernie Wright." Bernie's voice sounded edgy.

"Hey, Bernie, how're you holding up, buddy?" Amanda's voice was sympathetic but strong for Bernie. She hoped that their looking into the matter might give him some comfort. Bernie had often told Jake that he was a lucky man, but Bernie also knew that Jake was a special guy; he had to be to keep the interest of someone like Amanda.

"Well, I'm trying to concentrate on other things, but I keep thinking that I should be down there doing something. I feel helpless and useless here."

Amanda sensed the frustration in his voice. "Listen, Bernie, I know you feel like something more should be happening here, and frankly, I don't disagree. This Detective Tao is a piece of work, but I did manage to find out that Keith, Gail, and Taylor did pick up their luggage and probably hopped into either a rental car or had someone they knew pick them up. What I don't understand is how they just disappeared after that, but it has to have something to do with whoever picked them up."

Amanda took a breath and continued. "Do you know if they were meeting friends on the island? Think back. Did Gail or Taylor mention anything at all about the trip? For example, were they going anywhere special as soon as they arrived? Were they planning a hiking trip or a trip to see the volcano or anything on their own or with someone else?" There was a long pause. "Bernie, you still there? Jake, I think I lost the cell signal."

"No, Amanda, I'm still here," Bernie piped in quickly. "Sorry, I was just thinking. I have a room and computer set up here for Taylor, as you know, and I know I shouldn't have, but I started looking through her e-mails and her cached websites—you know, just to see if there were any clues whatsoever. I don't even know what I was looking for. I felt really guilty about it, but it's the first thing we do these days when investigating missing teens, so I thought, *Why wouldn't I do the same thing here, right?*" Bernie sounded like he was looking for approval, so Amanda nodded and then realized he couldn't see that, so she spoke quietly: "Bernie, you have to do what you have to do. Taylor is the most important thing in your life. She's not going to mind that you looked at her private stuff to try and find her."

"Well, then," he continued, and the words started to come out in chunks before Amanda realized Bernie was sobbing. "She was having an online relationship with some guy by the name of Carlos; I am sure that's not his real name. Nobody uses real names, do they? Anyway, the reason . . ." He choked back a sob. "The reason she reached out to this guy is because he was going through a split with his parents too, or so he says."

"Amanda, some of the things she said about me and Gail—I had no idea she was feeling that way." Then Bernie broke into long, shuddering sobs, and Amanda just let him go. Ever since he had been caught in the affair, guilt had eaten him up. He never meant for it to happen, but the stress of work combined with tension at home made him vulnerable that night. He loved Gail but felt so alone and misunderstood. Margarite seemed to know him and care.

When he quieted, Amanda spoke. "Bernie, our kids mean more to us than anything. When something goes astray, we often blame ourselves for what our kids are feeling, but they are individuals too. They make up their own minds, and at fifteen Taylor is a young adult. Kids do and say things because they are confused and don't understand now, but eventually they do. You and I know that. We have seen it a million times with teens, and we have experienced it ourselves in our own childhoods. Don't let it get to you now; she needs you to be strong." Amanda glanced over at Jake, who was driving like a maniac but managing to keep the ride smooth. *How does he do that?* she thought. "OK, Bernie, come on. What if anything in those e-mails and websites will help me here?"

"I don't know if any of this stuff will help. They talked about school and not having their dads around. There was a lot about favorite music and movies, but there were some things that seemed weird and unlike Taylor. For example, they talked about walking together in the 'other world.' Carlos talked about being spiritual and mentioned some prophecies. Taylor has always been grounded in reality, but they chatted about the end coming in 2012 and how they must be cleansed. Carlos mentioned how the 'island rituals were a door to paradise,' whatever that means. He said that he hoped to see her soon." Bernie sighed. "Amanda, the only thing I can think of is the link to the island. Could it be that there is something going on there that has to do with this island ritual thing?"

"Bernie, did you tell Detective Tao about this?"

"No, it seems weird but harmless enough to me. Do you think I should tell him?"

"Not right now. In fact, why don't you leave that piece of info with me, and the next time I speak to the detective I will mention it. Besides, he doesn't seem to care much for spiritual stuff. How long have they been e-mailing?"

"The e-mails started about two months after Gail and I divorced back in April. But the weird thing is, I don't find any communication between them on Facebook. It seems like direct e-mails are the way this Carlos guy wants to communicate, and perhaps text, but I haven't been able to access that yet.

"Well, that gives me a start," Amanda broke in. "Bernie, I am getting into a no-coverage area, so I'm gonna let you go. Don't read too much into all this just yet. Maybe this Carlos guy is a school friend. Whatever is going on, we'll find out. Keep your cell on." With that Amanda pressed END and turned to Jake.

"You're not going to believe this," Amanda said. She went on to give Bernie's side of the cell conversation to Jake, who kept his eyes on the road, but Amanda could see the concentration going on behind his eyes, and she knew Jake was connecting the dots.

CHAPTER 5

AMANDA HIT PAY DIRT AT THE FOURTH RENTAL-CAR COMPANY. "Yes, we have reported one of our cars stolen, rented by a Carlos Sirpit on December 26. He was supposed to have the car back yesterday afternoon, but he never showed up."

Carlos? Ha! Well, I guess some guys do use their real names, Amanda thought.

"But it's not his real name," interrupted Tanya the rental-company manager, who seemed overly bubbly for this time of the evening. "We found out it was a fake driver's license. The name does not exist in the Hawaiian database, and it was a Hawaiian driver's license."

"What kind of car was it?" Amanda inquired.

"Oh, a really nice sedan, a Mercedes 2002, but in mint condition. All black inside and out."

"Yeah, just the kind of car Keith would fall all over himself to have," Amanda mumbled.

"Who's Keith?" Bubbly jumped in.

"Uh, nobody. Listen, does anyone there know what the guy looks like? Did you happen to photocopy the driver's license he provided?" *Even a fake ID would have to match the picture to the person,* Amanda thought. *Maybe we can find out what this guy looks like.*

"Sorry, we just take down the license number. Smithy was working that shift, said the guy had a ball cap, dark glasses, and a Billabong T-shirt."

"Oh, like half the guys on the island," Amanda quipped. "Does Smithy remember anything else about the guy at all?"

"Nope, he's pretty old and can't remember what he had for breakfast most days."

"Well, thanks for your help." Amanda hung up irritably and called Detective Tao.

"Yes, yes, we have the plate number, make, model, etc. The car was found outside of Hilo on the Hawaii Belt Road near the Ola'a forest. No signs of struggle and no tracks except some leading back onto the road. Looks like the group got into another vehicle, except there were only two sets of foot-print tracks that we could find going back up to the road, two large sets. It's the rainy part of the island and tracks can stay imprinted for days. We don't know how long ago the car was abandoned. No bodies found in the general area for a four-mile radius. Their luggage was still in the trunk, along with a purse belonging to Gail Wright. Anything else you need to know, *Detective* Bannon?"

"No, Detective, and we both know I'm not a detective, but I appreciate the promotion in your mind."

"Well, you have certainly gotten further than most would have by now. Perhaps it's time we meet, Ms. Bannon. Since you seem to be sticking to this like cane syrup, we might as well be on the same team. Maybe you have information you can share with me that will help us to find your friends sooner."

Amanda started to get that funny churning feeling once again in her stomach. *OK,* she told herself. *Go with it. Something is not quite right with Detective Tao. Maybe he beats his wife or something, but right now you need him more than he needs you.*

"Fine, Detective. When and where? We just arrived in Hilo, and it's late. How about we meet for coffee, 7:00 a.m. at your headquarters?"

"No, Ms. Bannon. How about in twenty minutes at my headquar-ters?" With that he hung up the phone. Amanda looked at her cell phone incredulously. Then to Jake, "Don't get comfortable. We need to get to Hilo police headquarters in less than twenty minutes."

"Shit," was all Jake said as he grabbed the keys to the Viper.

They had just checked into the Castle Hilo hotel, and they were looking forward to rest and a fresh start in the morning. But now it looked like it could be a very long night.

CHAPTER 6

THE ROOM WAS SMALL AND DARK, WITH AN EARTHY SMELL TO IT. The walls were stone and dirt held together with mortar, and the only light was from the moonlight shining in through a tiny round window about ten feet up, just below the ceiling. Taylor was scared and hungry. It had been about two days, in her estimation, since she had seen her mom and Keith. She couldn't help but think the worst. She kept beating herself up, thinking that it was all her fault. If only she hadn't been so stupid.

All she wanted was for her mom and dad to get back together. This all went sideways. Keith was an idiot. He would always look her up and down when he arrived, and he had no clue how *uncool* he really was in his polo shirt from the '80s and his cargo pants. This was just supposed to help her mom see through Keith's act, but it wasn't supposed to put all their lives in danger. As soon as Taylor knew something was wrong she hid her phone in her sock, in case she would need it later to call for help or e-mail Carlos.

Taylor pulled out her cell phone and turned it on. It had a full battery but no reception. She had forgotten to turn her phone back on when she got off the airplane, which was good because it would have been dead by now. She had hidden it in her sock when she realized they'd been kidnapped, and there it had stayed until she was thrown into the dungeon two days ago. She checked it the first day, but there was no reception. There was still no reception. Although she was comforted by the artificial light, there was no use in wasting the battery, so she turned it off and slipped it back down her sock.

Just then she heard a key in the lock and the door slowly swung opened. A large man, whose head nearly touched the ceiling, filled the doorway. A glint of moonlight shone on the man's face. He had black eyes and ruddy skin with tattoos of snakes dancing on his face.

Taylor shivered and closed her eyes tight. *This has to be a nightmare*, she thought. *How could such a simple thing turn into this?* She could feel the presence of the hideous man in the room. The stale air seemed heated, an energy that she had not felt prior to his entrance. "What do you want?" she managed to squeak out with her eyes still shut. "Who are you and where is my mom? Please," she managed with a choke, "is my mom OK?"

A voice so soft that it seemed to be coming from within her replied, "You are the one, Taylor. Do not act like you are not responsible for your own destiny. You will do what is required." Taylor had no idea what this creep was talking about. He seemed to be in a zombie-like state. His voice, although soft, was deep and steady, and it terrified her. "The time has come. You must prepare yourself for the ceremony." The voice trailed off in a whisper that seemed to last for minutes, then coolness. Taylor slowly opened her eyes, and as they adjusted to the moonlight she glanced quickly to the closed door and around the empty room. For a moment she felt like she had imagined the whole encounter. Unfortunately, she knew better.

CHAPTER 7

THE POLICE HEADQUARTERS IN HILO WAS ON KAPIOLANI STREET AND WELL MAINTAINED. They arrived with two minutes to spare. Detective Tao was waiting on the front steps. Amanda knew it was him because he looked exactly like he sounded—irritated.

"You must be the Bannons," he said with a smirk. "Well, I was expecting Bonnie and Clyde, not a couple of jet-setters."

Amanda looked over at Jake and cringed at the Armani golf shirt tucked into Hugo Boss cargo shorts. *Oh well, you can never be too overdressed, right?* she thought.

"Well, Detective, we aren't here for a fashion show, so let's get down to business," Jake suggested.

"Let's take a walk," urged the detective. So they followed him around the corner of the building down a narrow path toward a grove of trees, where he stopped abruptly and turned to them. His face was obscured in the shadows where the moonlight's reach was softened.

"I know these are close friends of yours, and you just want to help. However, I do not want to have to worry about looking for two more missing people."

"Detective, I appreciate your concern," Amanda jumped in. "However, Jake and I have been—" The detective put up his hand to halt Amanda mid-sentence.

"Yes, yes, I know. You have both been involved in several cases. I have heard this already from the department, but this is not Canada, and the rules of engagement are different here. And, Ms. Bannon, regarding your gift, we will not rule out your *intuition;* just be aware that it is not something we will put a lot of faith in—we work with facts."

"Detective, if I may." Amanda waited for the detective to nod his go-ahead. "What we have learned so far is that the three missing individuals arrived at the Hilo airport on Air Canada. They were seen picking up their bags at the baggage claim area by another family that was sitting near them on the airplane. We feel that there must have been a car waiting for them already as the taxi-stand attendant working that day did not see them, nor was there a car rented under any of their names at any of the car-rental agencies." Amanda stopped and sucked in some air. The detective looked bored, since he knew all of this already, but she wanted him to hear everything in detail just in case the full picture triggered anything. "We spoke to Bernie Wright again and found out that his daughter was having some sort of online relationship with a guy named Carlos. We then found that a black Mercedes sedan had been rented through Aloha Rentals to a Carlos Sirpit, and, well, here we are."

Detective Tao gazed for a few moments over Amanda's head, then looked back down and said, "Yes, we have unfortunately seen an increase in these types of online connections and all the problems that go along with Internet relationships. I guess the old adage 'Don't talk to strangers' doesn't include Web chat."

Again the detective thought about how he had not allowed the Internet into his home, how his son Charlie had asked for a computer, like his friends had, and how he had explained to him that too many children were dying because of the Internet. Charlie didn't seem to make the connection, and Tao knew he would have to give in sooner or later; kids needed the Internet for school, research, and just about everything else these days. It was unfair to keep that advantage from Charlie, but for now, he felt better for doing so. His wife, of course, thought he was insane and bought herself an iPhone. "One of us has to live in the twenty-first century," she insisted.

Tao had a BlackBerry but used it strictly for work. He ignored the text messages his wife sent him and told her to call him at work for emergencies only. She was pretty good about it, calling him only once, when Charlie fell off the monkey bars at school and was taken to the hospital with a broken arm and a slight concussion. The cell phone was handy for these types of things, but he still loathed the Internet and refused to use it except when required for work.

Amanda caught the tired look that came across the detective's face and knew that he must be getting weary of the increase in Internet crimes against children. *For all its wonders, the Internet can be a dangerous place*, she thought.

"Yes, there seems to be a lack of judgment online. Jake and I will stay out of your way, Detective, but we will continue to follow our leads, and although we use some slightly unorthodox approaches, we have been successful to date," Amanda informed him.

"Just as long as I don't have to arrest you and as long as you remember this isn't your job. You have been given special privileges; that's all. And, oh, one last thing: we are not responsible for your safety. I would hate to see something happen to you. It is not the type of collateral damage we are looking for. Good evening to you both."

With that the detective strode off, leaving them standing in the alcove. Even though she could barely make him out in the darkness of night, Amanda could see Jake looking at her with his raised eyebrows.

* * *

Amanda and Jake headed back to the car. "Jake, I don't like this. I feel like we need to do something more tonight. We've let too much time go by already."

"What are you talking about, Amanda? We just found out about all of this, and here we are in the middle of it. What are you saying? You don't need any sleep? It's eight o'clock. What good will you be exhausted and not thinking straight?" Amanda glanced over at Jake until he finally gave in.

"OK, fine, where to?" he said as he put the car into gear and backed out of the parking lot at the Hilo police station.

"Let's take a drive up the highway," she said, smiling. "I have a feeling the police may have missed something along that road."

"You mean something that only you can see," Jake said, knowing Amanda was sensing something, as he took full advantage of the Viper's ability.

The highway had a sharp, beautiful look as the lush green vegetation glimmered in the soft moonlight. Once again Amanda marveled at the beauty of the Big Island. These islands certainly were gems floating in the warm Pacific. No wonder everyone she talked to spoke about buying a home in Maui or Kauai and about retiring to a place surrounded by ocean, blue sky, and miles of beaches to explore. Island living was what Jake and Amanda had dreamed about for most of their adult lives. And now here they were, but it wasn't quite what she had expected—driving at night on a deserted highway in the most sinister part of the island, searching for clues about their missing friends. "What the hell are we doing out here?" Amanda blurted out.

"Don't even go there, Amanda. This was all your idea, remember?" Jake growled. "I'm just the luggage boy."

"Jake, you are the most resourceful, wonderful, intelligent luggage boy I know." Amanda grinned. Jake knew that was about as close to a thank-you as Amanda would get, and it came from the heart, so he threw the Viper into sixth gear.

"What a piece of shit, Amanda. Couldn't you get an Aston Martin DBS or something with balls?"

Amanda grimaced. "Sorry honey, they were all out—of Aston Martins, not balls. Do your best."

Following the map, they came to the area where the kidnapper's car was found, according to Detective Tao. They got out of the Viper and walked up the highway a bit. After a while Jake called ahead to Amanda: "Anything?"

"Ummm, no, not yet." Amanda strolled up a bit farther. Suddenly she started to feel it, the tightening in her abdomen. The feeling of anxiety forced her to slowly move farther inland, toward the slope and down into the forest.

"Amanda," Jake shouted, alarmed, "be careful. That's steep. You could—" Too late. Jake ran toward her as she slid and then tumbled head-first into the ditch beside the road.

Jake was there instantly, climbing down and kneeling beside Amanda. He took her in his arms and whispered in her ear, "Dead or alive?"

"Alive," she moaned. "I think I may have sprained something, but I am still trying to figure out what it is." Jake smiled and picked her up, then gently put her down on her feet. "Something happened here, Jake, and it feels bad."

Jake shone his pilot LED flashlight around the area. "Which way?" he asked.

Amanda stood for a moment and pointed. "Over there, by that brush." Jake held Amanda by the arm and they gingerly stepped through the long wet grass and moved around some small rocks. Jake was holding the flashlight, waving it slowly back and forth in front of them. "Stop!" Amanda said sharply. "Back—just a bit to the right, where you just went over. There, see it?" Jake squinted. There was a shiny glint of metal.

He quickly walked over and picked it up. "Looks like a piece of a memory board, for a cell phone—one that has been snapped or crushed. Maybe someone accidentally stepped on it."

"Or purposely stepped on it," Amanda chimed in. "Seems like a funny place to find something like that, don't you think?"

"Yeah, but why just a piece of it, Amanda—why not the whole phone? Where's the rest of it?"

"Well, maybe whoever crushed the phone and collected the broken pieces missed one."

"Yup, I guess I didn't think anyone would take the time to clear the evidence so well during a kidnapping out in the boonies," Jake mused.

"That's because you're one of the good guys and it's hard for you to think like a bad guy." Amanda smiled. "Now let's get out of this ditch; it's giving me the creeps."

CHAPTER 8

CARLOS DIDN'T SMILE, BUT HE FELT GOOD. Everything was going just as he had planned; he would be well rewarded for his work. *It really hadn't been that difficult*, he thought. *Taylor was vulnerable and open to just about anything. People who allow their children too much freedom set them up to be taken in by anything that will give them a way out. They will now have to deal with the consequences of their actions.*

When Carlos was a child, his father taught him discipline, to learn to accept pain as part of who he was. Carlos was not allowed to indulge in normal activities, as other children did. He did not have television or toys. His father taught him that hard work was fulfilling; play was not. Carlos worked in the fields on their farm from morning until dark. He cleaned the stalls, fed the animals, mended fences, chopped wood, collected eggs, milked the cow, brushed the horses, baled the hay, and kept the dogs. He even had to clean the house. He did not go to school like other children. His father warned him that other children learned nothing of value; they followed false gods and idolized movie stars, mere men and women put on a screen. He told him that fame and glamour made you fat and unworthy. His father taught him everything he needed to know about religion, his own fundamentalist version of Christianity that shunned anything of the world and heaped guilt upon Carlos, guilt that could only be paid for through hard work, self-denial, and repeated discipline, which included the shedding of his blood. He was never worthy enough. He wouldn't let Carlos cut his dark, shaggy hair, believing he belonged to some sort of chosen race. He kept Carlos out of school, teaching him reading, writing, and arithmetic at home. "The basics are all you need, along with your instinct," claimed his father.

Carlos was allowed to go to town on occasion when his father required help with loading supplies. These times were few and far between. However, they meant the world to Carlos. The supply store they visited was run by a small man by the name of Aaron, and he had a daughter slightly younger than Carlos. She had dark hair and big brown eyes, and Carlos couldn't take his eyes off of her while he was there. One time while visiting, his father asked Carlos to finish loading the supplies while he went out back with Aaron to discuss some business. Carlos was left alone with the girl, who was adding up lists of numbers at the counter. Carlos went in and out of the store, loading the truck. Each time he came in he looked across the room at her, until one time she looked up directly at him and smiled. His heart nearly burst, and he tripped and fell to the grounds with his supplies. She giggled at him, and it was the sweetest sound he had ever heard. On the few occasions when he came back, the two of them innocently spoke a few words, generally producing a stern look from their two fathers.

Carlos was made to endure pain on a regular basis. His father would often whip him with horse reins until his back was ripped and bloody. When he was younger, he cried, but over the years he could bear the pain without crying. By the time he was seventeen, Carlos passed his father's height of six foot two and had uncommon strength and stamina due to the hard work and beatings he had endured.

One afternoon, while his father was in town getting supplies, a man carrying a Bible walked up to Carlos as he was coming in from the field. Guessing the boy to be older than he was, the man asked Carlos if it was his farm. Carlos explained he lived there with his father. The man claimed to be a preacher from a town just south of their farm, and he was looking for those who might want to ready themselves to enter the gates of heaven. Carlos had never heard anyone speak of such things, or met anyone who spoke so gently. And the man seemed to look right through Carlos's eyes into his soul. He asked the man what he meant, and soon they were sitting under the big elm tree on the farm in deep conversation about this man's God and the matters covered in the book he carried.

After a while, as they sat under the tree, a dark shadow engulfed them. Carlos squinted into the sunlight and saw his father standing over them. Carlos jumped up. *Had it been that long?* he thought. His father had not been due back for hours. He could not believe that the time had gone by so quickly. They had been so engrossed in the discussion they had not heard the truck pull into the driveway or his father walk right up to them. The man with the gentle voice stood and put his hand out. "Reverend Brian McDowen." Carlos's father slapped the man's hand away and pointed to the road without saying a word. The reverend saw the hate in his eyes and decided it was best to leave. The reverend's voice quivered as he told Carlos to keep the faith and stay strong. He grabbed his Bible and walked quickly, almost jogging, to his old car. He sped away, leaving a trail of dust floating silently in the air behind him.

Carlos was used to his father's anger and beatings. Sometimes it was worse than others, but he had only seen his father this angry a couple times before, like the time when Carlos had mustered up the courage to ask for a new pair of boots. His father went into a rant about the influence of the townspeople and their materialistic wants. He took Carlos to the barn and beat him with the horse reins until he was exhausted. He told Carlos the sins of the world were upon him and only through the shedding of his blood could there be cleansing. This time, however, Carlos saw something very different in his father's eyes. It was a rage so fierce Carlos was not sure what would happen next.

"I didn't . . . ," Carlos began, but that was all he got out before his father hammered his fist into Carlos's face, breaking his nose and dropping him to his knees. His father then kicked him in the stomach, knocking the wind out of him. Carlos blacked out at that point, moving in and out of consciousness as his body was tied to the elm tree and whipped with the reins. He was jolted to full consciousness when the branding iron seared the flesh on his back. Intoxicated by rage, his father kept it up till late evening. Finally, around midnight, his father was exhausted and went to the house to crash, leaving Carlos tied to the tree, almost dead.

The warmth of the late-morning sun aroused Carlos from unconsciousness. He heard the screen door slam and shuddered. His father came out with a large knife. He cut the ropes that held Carlos and let his limp body drop to the ground. His father went to the well and drew some water. He put a small cup of water and a piece of bread next to where Carlos lay. His face was swollen and his body hurt so much he could barely swallow. His swollen nose had stopped bleeding, but he could barely breathe between bites. He heard the truck start and then drive away. He knew his father would be away for a while; he always left the next day after his mindless rages. Carlos finished his bread and dragged himself to the well for some more water. Drawing the bucket was excruciatingly painful, but he desperately needed to drink. Three cupfuls later, he could manage to stand enough to stumble to the house. He dragged himself to his bedroom, packed his only other two pairs of pants and his one good shirt, and left his childhood home. He managed to half walk and half crawl down the dirt driveway and onto the main roadway. It took him an hour to make it down the road about half a mile when a small red truck stopped. Carlos tried to look as nonchalant as he could. An old man asked through a half-rolled-down window, "Do you want a ride? 'Cause you look like you need one." Carlos slowly climbed into the truck while the old man was asking in a friendly voice, "Where you off to?" As Carlos turned toward him, the old man's face fell and his mouth gaped open. "Boy, you need a hospital!" Then everything faded to black.

*   *   *

When he woke up he was in a bed, something he had never experienced. He always slept on blankets on the floor. He could hear voices outside his hospital room. A kind-looking woman in a white dress walked over and put her fingers on the inside of his wrist and looked at her watch. She noticed that he was staring at her, and she said, "Well, good morning, stranger. Glad you are awake. Maybe we can get some answers from you."

Carlos looked in alarm at the tubes coming out from his arms and asked, "Where am I?"

"Well, you are at the general hospital in Benton, and we are taking good care of you. It looks like you have endured a lot. The doctor will have some questions for you. I will be right back."

Carlos looked around the room. He had never seen anything like it. There were white bedsheets and curtains. The bed across from him was empty, and a third one next to him held a skinny old man who was fast asleep. His father had told him about hospitals. He said it was where Carlos's mother had died, giving birth to him. *This is a place of death*, he thought. *I need to leave.*

He could hear the voice of the woman who had just spoken to him talking with a man outside in the hallway. "Doctor," the woman said, "he doesn't seem to know where he is."

"The old man thought he had been in a car accident, but I am pretty sure that's not the case. Most of the bruises seem to have been made by a fist or stick or pipe or something. And the S-shaped burns look like they were made by a branding iron. Someone did this to him, and although he is a large guy, I am guessing he is no older than twenty."

"What are you going to do?" The woman sounded concerned.

"Well, the best thing to do is ask him to tell us what happened to him, if he can remember." Carlos heard them come into his room, and he closed his eyes. The doctor gently touched his arm. Carlos did not respond. "Well, he must have passed out from the medication again. Let me know as soon as he wakes. We need to find out what happened and report this to the local authorities."

Carlos's heart beat rapidly. *Local authorities?* he thought. His father had warned him about the local authorities. He had to get out of there.

The nurse came in several times throughout the day and into the evening. Each time Carlos pretended to be in a deep sleep. She finally left and was replaced by a different woman in a white hat. That night, when it was dark and the old man next to him was snoring loudly, Carlos clenched his teeth and pulled the tubes out of his arm. He then snuck over to the door and peered down the hallway. To the left, it was dark except for the nurses' station, which was lit up. A nurse was sitting and reading a book, facing the other way. To the right, there was nothing between him and an illuminated exit sign. He slowly hobbled down the hall and quietly pushed the door open, gently closing it behind him. He struggled down three flights of stairs. At the bottom was another door with a small window in it. Through the window Carlos could make out a tree bathed in moonlight. He quickened his pace, pushed the bar across the door, and then fled into the cool night.

CHAPTER 9

TAYLOR SHIVERED IN THE DARK CELL. She wondered if she was going to starve to death in this cold, dank place. She thought about all the issues with her parents: how upset she was over their split, how much she disliked Keith, and how trivial all of that seemed now that her family was in total danger. And it was her fault they were there.

She remembered the first time Carlos had e-mailed her. She knew that it was dangerous to start an online relationship. Her mom constantly warned her about making Internet friends, but his poem about finding strength in pain was so moving. He opened up to her so quickly about his dad's abuse toward him and how his mom left when he was young. She knew she could help him.

How was she to know that coming to the Big Island to meet Carlos would turn into a nightmare? She had trusted him with all her secrets about her parents and their split. She believed he was her true soul mate. He commiserated with her when her father missed their shopping trip. He understood her disgust over how Keith would leer at her and treated her with indifference when her mother wasn't around. Carlos was different, or so she thought. He was very intense and deep. He thought about more than just cars and sports. He was even thoughtful enough to remember her birthday, and he had sent a driver in a Mercedes—a "real beauty," as Keith had put it—when they stepped out of the airport terminal and saw a very tall, dark driver looking sharp in a black suit and chauffeur's hat, holding open the door for them. Taylor remembered how Keith was in the car before the driver had the luggage in the trunk. "Wow, that's terrific service," he had almost sung. "I got us the top-shelf package, Gail. I didn't know it included a car," he had said, grinning like a fool. Now Taylor would give anything to see Keith's foolish grin again. When they got in the back, Keith yelled up to the driver, "Ummm, we're headed to the—," but the driver cut him off and, in a low, soft voice, said, "I have all the details, Mr. Stevens. All of you just sit back and relax. There is a complimentary bottle of champagne chilling in the ice bucket. It is a bit of a ride, so sit back and enjoy."

Taylor remembered how the driver's voice was a bit of a monotone, like he was reading from a script, but, then, at the time she'd simply thought he had been told exactly what to say when driving VIPs. She remembered feeling like a superstar, sitting in the back of the Mercedes on their way to a great vacation, and on the way to meet her newfound soul mate, Carlos. He wrote to her about making sacrifices and having a bigger view of life and why we are here. No more pain for either of them when they reached paradise together. They used secret code words. Carlos had even promised her that he would set up something to "fix" her problem with Keith. He said he would use their secret religion to gain control and change the relationship so that Keith and her mom would split up. That her mom would realize the only man for her was Taylor's dad. That he would send a car and that she should just play along and enjoy the ride. But this was not what was supposed to happen; it had all gone wrong. If only she had not convinced her mom to let her try some champagne. She remembered calling to her mom when everything started to blur and turn dark after she took the last sip. What if they hadn't gotten in the car? What if she had never started that stupid Internet friendship in the first place? What if she had just told her parents how she was really feeling? She couldn't help wishing things had been different, but nothing could ease the sick feeling she had in the pit of her stomach. She knew that Carlos, the one person she thought she could trust, had something to do with all this. She knew that she had something to do with it too. She hoped that her dad realized they were missing and was searching for her, but even that small hope faded as she looked around again at the awful black space.

CHAPTER 10

"**Well, what do you make of all of it?**" Jake looked quizzically at Amanda.

"Let's look at the whole thing again," she said, taking a deep breath. "The Wrights split up. Taylor meets someone by the name of Carlos online. He claims to understand her issues and they become close friends after about half a year. He invites her to Hawaii—probably where he lives and not just some fun destination he pulled out of the air. Then Taylor convinces Gail and Keith that the Big Island would be a great place to spend New Year's. Keith loves the idea—anything for a party. For the first time since her divorce Gail sees a glint of joy in her daughter's eyes, so she's all for it. Keith books a package vacation, since it was the most inexpensive way he'd found to do the trip. He is excited when they arrive and have a car waiting to take them to the hotel. Enamored of the Mercedes, Keith does not ask for credentials, and they all hop into the back and then disappear. The car is found deserted in the middle of the Belt Road, Route 11, just outside of Volcano National Park, close to the entry for the Ola'a rain forest, with all of the luggage and Gail's purse still inside. There is no sign of a struggle, so I am guessing they either went willingly or were carried by two large men, as the pair of footprints suggests. Finally, we find a piece of a cell phone memory board that could belong to one of the bad guys but more likely to Keith or Taylor, since, according to the detective, Gail's phone was in her purse. Since the tracks show they were going back to the highway, it's likely they hitched a ride with another vehicle. But we don't know if they continued going south or headed back to Hilo. It was highly unlikely that anyone spotted anything at that time of the evening until the car was finally reported to the police by that trucker, abandoned at the side of the road."

"So that leaves us exactly . . . nowhere," Jake said, looking glum.

"Yup, except for one thing." Amanda's eyes grew wide. "They continued down the highway, going south." Jake was about to ask her how she knew that but then remembered just to accept that she was right.

"OK, south we go," he said as they got into the car and headed down the highway.

CHAPTER 11

CARLOS KNEW THAT TAYLOR WAS SCARED, AND SHE SHOULD HAVE
BEEN. The time was coming. Even though he knew time was short and he
had to prepare, he wanted to hold off until the full moon—January 7 to 9—
when the offering would have the highest value. Her sacrifice would be the
great catalyst that would usher him into the new world, where he would be
renewed and removed from the pain he felt from his childhood. He would
be elevated to the next level, and when the end arrived, he would be master
of his newly found domain. He would be given powers beyond his imagination, and his flight to the spiritual side would be complete. Liag had said so,
and he owed his salvation to Liag, who had shown him the way to the truth.
He had waited for this moment since he found out the truth about himself
and his father. If only his father had understood that truth was the answer.

As Carlos was preparing the altar, he allowed himself to drift back
again, back to the night he slipped away from the hospital. After leaving
the hospital, he realized how little he knew of the outside world. He wondered why the old man had taken him to that place, why the people had
helped him. His face was bandaged, and he had some type of plastic cloth
taped around his midsection. The wounds on his back had been cleaned and
stitched together with some thick, black thread. *The people seemed kind*, he
thought. *They wanted to help*, but Carlos was afraid of the tubes in his arms.
He felt better after resting there, but he also knew that he didn't belong

there. Carlos decided to go back home. *Sure, it's a tough life*, he reasoned. *But he's my father, and he's taken care of me since my mother died.* Carlos thought about how his mother had died giving him life and felt guilty for causing his father so much pain. He decided to ask his father for forgiveness, to promise never to speak to anyone again.

Carlos recognized the roads that led back to the farm. He fell asleep for a few hours in a field that he had to cross. The warm midday sun beating down on his face woke him up. He started walking again, and he reached his father's farm by the afternoon. His father's truck was not in its usual place, and Carlos knew he must be out taking a load of grain to the mill, as he often did at that time of day. He found the key to the house on top of the door frame where he had seen his father put it several times over the years. He opened the back door and entered the house. It smelled stale, and a very light layer of dust had settled over everything. He realized that he must have been in the hospital longer than he had thought. When Carlos was home, he kept the house relatively clean, wiping down the kitchen and main room each night before bed. He could see the evidence of his father's usual quick breakfast of toast and a cup of coffee. His father never ate more than he absolutely had to. He never indulged. The most he would allow himself was a bowl of oatmeal on occasion. There were crumbs on the counter and a mug with a quarter cup of black coffee next to the sink. Carlos's relationship with his father had always seemed surreal. It always felt like he was standing outside his own body watching a small boy grow up. But for some reason seeing the mess made his father seem more human. Carlos went upstairs and stared down the narrow corridor to the door of his father's bedroom. It was closed, just as it had always been, as far back as he could remember. He slowly walked toward the door. He felt like he was not in control of his body. He watched his hand reach out toward the doorknob. *What are you doing? You cannot go in there!* he screamed in his head. Although his father had never said not to, ever since he was very young he knew never to open that door. In fact, he rarely came upstairs, having slept in the barn for most of his young life. Ever since he was a small boy, he had been curious about his father. He thought that all his father's secrets were hidden in that room. Now, as though someone else were in his body, controlling his hand, he slowly turned the knob and swung the door open.

The room was dark. The shades were drawn. When his eyes adjusted, he was disappointed by how ordinary the room seemed. There was nothing special there. The dingy gray sheets were crumpled, and a solitary pillow was lying on the floor. He walked over to the window and drew the shade up halfway to let in the daylight. He turned to look at the bed. It was smaller than he had expected. In fact, he was sure his father could not fit properly in it. He was too tall. A thicker layer of dust covered the few pieces of furniture. His eyes wandered around the room as his heart beat fiercely in his chest. He moved over to the dresser, an old piece that badly needed to be refinished. There were some papers on top and a few letters. He could read fairly well and knew that some of these were demanding money from his father. He slowly pulled open the top drawer and his heart continued to pound. There were a few items in this drawer: a pen, some batteries, and a flashlight. There were some bullets but no gun, and a piece of paper with a photo clipped to it. He had a searing sensation in his gut. He was drawn to the photo. He removed the paper and stared at the photograph. He immediately recognized his much younger father next to a plain-looking woman with rich brown skin. She was holding a baby in her arms. He stared, unable to believe what he was seeing. The woman's eyes, big and dark, black in fact, were the same eyes he saw each day when he looked into the mirror. There was no mistaking it. She was Carlos's mother.

CHAPTER 12

TAYLOR WAS COLD AND HUNGRY AND SCARED. Worse, she had to go to the bathroom. She could make out the bucket in the corner of the room. She had already had to use it once, but that didn't make it any easier this time. She thought about what might have crawled in there since the last time she went. She had to figure a way to get her family out of this mess. Carlos was supposed to be her friend. He said he would have a car waiting for them when they arrived, and of course Keith would assume it had something to do with the cheap package he had managed to get them. When Carlos had said that he would use their secret religion to take care of Keith, she thought he meant he would give him a rash or something and her mom an anti-love potion. Now it looked like he had set her up too. Tears welled in Taylor's eyes, and she began to silently weep in the dark. *How could she be so stupid?* she kept asking herself over and over. He said he would have a car waiting for them when they arrived. But why would Carlos want to have her and her family kidnapped?

Her only hope was that her dad would be all over this. He was expecting her call on New Year's Eve. She had missed her night to stay up and call her dad as she had promised. *He probably has an entire division on a search-and-rescue mission already*, she thought. *But who was the crazy-looking guy with all the tattoos, and what did he have to do with Carlos?*

Taylor could barely breathe. She couldn't help thinking that she had broken the one rule her mother had always taught her: don't talk to strangers. She had screwed up.

CHAPTER 13

AS HE MOVED ABOUT, SETTING CANDLES AROUND THE ROOM, CAR-
LOS THOUGHT BACK TO THE DAY HE FOUND OUT THAT HIS MOTHER
WAS ALIVE. He remembered the shock that he had not caused her death
taking his breath away. A tear slowly trickled down the side of his face. He
quickly wiped it away. *No time for weakness*, he reminded himself. He had to
complete the steps. The sacrifice wouldn't be accepted if he did not follow
the sacred procedures. He continued with his task at hand, but he allowed
himself to slip back into his memories once more. All those years ago, he
had stared at the photo in his father's room and then slowly unfolded the
paper attached to the photo. The note was addressed to Henry, his father's
first name. The note simply stated: *I cannot stay with you. I cannot take care
of the baby. Please take good care of Carlos.* There was no signature, no name,
no nothing. She was gone. All Carlos's life, his father had told him that his
mother died in childbirth. All his life, his father had beaten him mercilessly
in order to cleanse him of the sin of taking his mother's life. All his life,
his father had lied to him and made him feel unending guilt and sadness
because his mother was gone. And while he had blamed himself all along,
she had left of her own accord. His mother had left because of his father, not
because of him. Her last request was for his father to take care of him. Now
he would take care of his father. Carlos suddenly became filled with rage. It
was burning through his veins like searing liquid. Then he heard the distinct

sound of his father's truck pull up in the driveway. He knew that if his father found him in his room, he would finish him. It was time for Carlos to take back some of the life his father had beaten out of him.

The front door opened. Carlos's breathing became shallow and rapid. He could not be found just standing there in his father's bedroom. He heard his father climbing the stairs. He quickly closed the dresser drawer and put the photo in his pocket. He quietly squeezed into the closet and tried to close the door. Due to his size, he had to leave it open a crack. His father entered the room slowly and looked at the half-open window shade, then ran his hand through his hair. He slowly pulled a handgun out of his jacket pocket and threw it on the bed. He slid his jacket off and tossed it on the chair next to the window. He walked over to the window and pulled the shade back down to its original position. Carlos held his breath as his father walked back over to the dresser, gently pulled open the top drawer, stared into it, and moved some items aside. Adrenaline coursed through Carlos's veins. He couldn't feel any pain anymore as his father slowly walked to the bed. Before Carlos knew what had happened, his father had picked up the gun and spun quickly to face the closet door.

"I know you are here," he said quietly. "I sensed it as soon as I walked in the house. You cannot hide from me any longer. You should have never come back." Before he had taken a complete step toward the closet door, Carlos burst out and was upon his father like an animal, knocking him to the ground. He could not control the rage that had been seething in his soul all these long years. He pounded his father's face and head with his massive fists. All the hurt and pain and anger was being released in full force. Nothing could stop him—not the agonized screams of his father, not the memory of his mother's face, not the blood splattering on the walls, not anything on this earth—nothing.

CHAPTER 14

"AMANDA, WE'VE BEEN DRIVING FOR NEARLY A FRIGGING HOUR HERE. Are you sure this is the right way? You are allowed to be wrong once in a blue moon, you know." The sarcasm was heavy now, and Amanda wanted to give him a jab from her side of the car, but instead she smiled her best and brightest smile.

"Well, darling, why don't we try your suggestion? Oh, yeah, you don't have one, do you?"

"Oh, but you are wrong there, my love." Jake smiled equally brilliantly. "My suggestion is to file a flight plan directly back to Honolulu and let the authorities work this one out."

Amanda looked hurt, then she leaned over and jabbed Jake in the arm with a quick sucker punch. "Ouch! OK, OK, we'll do it your way for the billionth time!" Jake rubbed his arm vigorously. "That's gonna leave a mark."

"Good," she shot back. "Hold on." Amanda jolted upright. "Turn back."

"What? Right now?" Jake asked incredulously.

"Yes, yes, about half a kilometer. Go, go, Jake, hurry!" Amanda's eyes were wide, and Jake knew better than to crack jokes now. She was on to something, and he knew that it would be an important clue or breakthrough in the case. He turned around and slowly crept along in order not to miss what Amanda was looking for. He made his way back until Amanda said, "OK, pull over. Right there. See it?"

Jake strained his eyes. "See what?"

"Right there, Jake, a trail right through those trees, between those two large, tangled bushes. It's like a natural path."

Jake looked more closely at the formation of the brush and trees. He strained his eyes and turned on his imagination. Then, there it was, right in front of him. It looked like the door to a death trap to Jake. If he hadn't been told what to look for, he never would have known it existed. "Wow, that's cool. If you really use your imagination, you're right, there is something there. So, you think this leads us to the gang?"

"Don't be such a wiseass. I am telling you, this is it. At least that is the feeling I am getting right now."

"Well, it leads us to something," said Jake. *Either the bad guys or a wild boar or both*, he thought. "Amanda, I don't know about this. It's late and it's dark. Do you think it's a good idea to just walk into what might be a hostile environment without a plan?"

"We have a plan and our stuff." She motioned to the backpacks in the back of the car, which contained their usual array of adventure items. Jake had insisted they leave them in the car and not the hotel . . . just in case. And they each had a handgun that they had carried everywhere since the incident in Chicago when Amanda had been unnaturally drawn into danger by her gift. She'd had a strong feeling that a woman was in danger and ended up getting jumped in an ally. The woman got away, and Amanda was able to escape by using her pepper spray, but ever since then Jake had insisted that she carry a piece at all times. Amanda carried a small snub-nose Smith & Wesson M&P .357 Magnum with a speed loader. Jake, the techno-geek, carried a composite Glock G20 10mm Auto. They also had their radios, climbing gear, and underwater breathing devices. And in a plastic bag with a humidity pack were a couple of Cuban Habanos, something you couldn't easily get in the U.S., but there were plenty in Canada.

"OK, we have our stuff, but what's the plan?" Jake looked tired, and Amanda could tell he was in no mood to banter, so she got right to it.

"Well, first of all, we don't know what this is all about. Bernie has not had any demands for a ransom. So we have to assume this is something else.

Most kidnappings are about money or drugs or, worse, they are the random acts of psychotic individuals. But even in those cases, most predators know the individual or individuals they are going after. It is usually planned and not something they do just on a whim."

Jake nodded. He knew Amanda wasn't trying to teach him something he already knew, but saying the facts out loud was her way of working through the details of the case to put things in order. Jake knew that by listening he was in fact helping her to fit the pieces of the puzzle together.

Amanda took a deep breath and continued. "I am going to guess that no ransom means no money or drugs, and because the suitcases and purse were left in the car, we can rule robbery out. So we are left with our favorite contestant: the deranged psycho or psycho savant." She held up her hand as Jake opened his mouth. "I know, this is the one option you were hoping against, but the logic is just pointing that way right now."

"No, that's not what I was going to say at all," Jake cut in. "Deranged psychos are my favorite." He rolled his eyes. "I know 'cause I live with one."

"Oh, ha, ha, just like I married you for comedic relief," she shot back. "Let me finish. So the last thing is, if this path leads to some psycho's lair, chances are it is not going to be an easy target. He's probably got some sick plans. I get the feeling he has planned out contingencies, just in case. So along with the typical dangers of hiking through basically a jungle in the middle of the night, we also need to watch for traps. This wasn't just an impromptu kidnapping."

"Well, it might have been. Maybe he was a Boy Scout in his youth, Amanda, and we may just walk into a bunch of lean-tos and a wild boar roasting on a spit."

"Nope," Amanda said defiantly, "not a chance. That path took weeks, maybe months to create, depending on how far into the jungle it goes." She crossed her arms over her chest and stuck out her chin in stubborn defiance, convinced that her instincts were right, again.

"OK, so now that you have it all figured out, what's the plan? Do we fly in there like Jet Li and take them down in hand-to-hand combat?"

"Well, you can do that, Jet. I plan to camouflage myself and crawl on my belly, scout out the place, find their weak spot, see if we can figure out where the victims are being held, and plan the attack with the least amount of collateral damage. Are you in?"

"Sounds good to me. I'll get the black paint and our packs. You do the makeup, girlfriend."

CHAPTER 15

CARLOS WAS RELIEVED THAT CHAPTER OF HIS LIFE WAS OVER, AND
HE WAS LOOKING FORWARD TO ANOTHER TRANSITION. He was fin-
ished setting up the altar and studied his plans. He had outlined the sequence
of the rituals, how everything would flow from one step to the next. He had
studied the ancient practice of voodoo, learning all he could about the religion in order to be a worthy servant. He knew he must learn to serve and to
honor the ancient ways. He must not be afraid to make sacrifices. Carlos had
spent his life making sacrifices. It came very easily to him. However, he knew
it would not be easy for the girl. *Has she figured it out yet?* he wondered. *Did
she realize that he was the one she had connected with all this time and that he
had tried to show her the way to the spiritual world?*

He had carefully drawn her into discussing ancient rituals, connecting her to the various worlds and truths of the religion. He mentioned the
prayer chants, the incense offerings, the animal sacrifices. She told him she
had read in the Bible that blood was necessary for atonement. Carlos was
careful never to mention virgin sacrifice in their conversations, but he figured she knew. She seemed to understand and even seemed eager to enter
another world and be free from the pain and suffering in this one. When he
met with her, though, he saw the raw fear in her eyes.

Maybe it had been a game to her. She may not have truly realized the
consequences. Still, Carlos felt no pity for the girl. Sacrifices had to be made,

and she had been presented to him by Liag, who had promised him a safe place to rest his soul. Carlos was suddenly tired. He felt like he could lie down and sleep for days. But he knew there was no time. He had to finish the next steps in preparing the altar. The ceremonial room had to be ready, clean, and decorated. He was finished with the candles and cleaning but still had to drape the altar and finish his prayers. Soon it would be time to offer up the girl, and then he would be able to rest eternally.

CHAPTER 16

DETECTIVE TAO SAT IN QUIET CONTEMPLATION AS HE GAZED OUT HIS OFFICE WINDOW INTO THE DARKNESS. He knew he should really slip home for some rest. His wife had been harping about how he spent too much time at the office and was missing their nine-year-old son's growing up. Tao was going to turn the big Five-O this year and was far from retiring, but he was getting tired of the game. He had quickly moved up through the ranks to become a detective at the young age of forty-five. He did not regret his decision to take the job, but he did regret waiting to have children with his wife. Now Angie was forty-five. They had tried desperately to have another child after Charlie was born to give him a playmate. Finally, though, the risk associated with getting pregnant at a late stage in life outweighed the need for a second child, so Tao had himself fixed. Tao's own mother had gotten a hysterectomy, and he never forgot how she had changed. He felt she was not at peace with herself when she died, and because of that he had always felt like he was not at peace. *Nevertheless, life goes on*, he thought, and his only regret was that he should have spent more time with Charlie. They needed the extra money the promotion had brought, but not the extra work and responsibility.

Money wasn't a problem now, but they had to budget well. By the time they saved and scraped enough to cover their mortgage and car payments and put Charlie through school, they would have just a little left to invest for their retirement. *By the time we're ready for retirement, we'll be too old and wasted to enjoy the few remaining years we have left, unlike the Bannons,* he thought, not without envy. Like swallowing a pill without water, he had a hard time taking in the research on that couple. He wanted to hate them for their good fortune but really could not. They had worked hard for their lifestyle and gave to many good causes, something Tao would love to do if he could ever get ahead. How he wanted to have their money, even if just for a day. He wanted to set a good example for Charlie, but it seemed there was never more than enough to make it to the next paycheck.

The Bannons were certainly a piece of work. Detective Tao admired their business prowess but didn't like them meddling in police business. Even though they had a good record with helping Canadian authorities track leads and bring closure to some tough cases, he knew that more often than not civilian involvement meant more people to rescue. He did not want to work with them, but he gave them some leeway since they were friends of the RCMP officer whose family was missing. The reality of the situation was that it would soon be the fourth day that these people had been missing, and the chance of their being found alive was rapidly shrinking. He figured the case was about to go from a rescue mission to a recovery of the bodies. He hoped to close the case before spring break so he'd have a chance to take Charlie to Disneyland. He'd been saving for the vacation for a while, and this year might work. He did not want to be so cold about it, but he had to think about his family too. Besides, these cases happened all the time. Then he thought about how the Bannons could probably afford Disneyland vacations every year. Tao had a jealous lump in his throat again. *Stop it*, he told himself. *If these people and their money, and her funny intuition, can help solve this case, then you can take Charlie to Disneyland. If this thing drags on, you can expect to spend the next several months on the hunt for three bodies in the jungle.* With that he suddenly felt the need to connect with Amanda Bannon and find out where they were.

CHAPTER 17

AMANDA FELT A VIBRATION IN HER POCKET AND QUICKLY PULLED OUT HER BLACKBERRY AND OPENED IT UP BEFORE MICHAEL JACKSON DECIMATED THE QUIET NIGHT. She reminded herself to change the setting to vibrate once she hung up. Although there was probably nobody within earshot, she did not want to take the chance that there might be sentries close by on the watch. They still had no idea of the size of the group or the capability of the individual who had kidnapped their friends.

"Hello," she said quietly into the phone.

"Ms. Bannon?" Detective Tao said in a sharp tone.

"Yes, Detective." She motioned to Jake to hold off entering the rain forest while she appeased the detective with whatever he needed.

"Ms. Bannon, I am about to leave the office and wanted to make sure you didn't need anything before I left."

Hmmm, this is an interesting change of attitude, thought Amanda. *Wonder what's up.* "Well, there really isn't anything, Detective. I do want you to know that Jake and I took a ride up to the area where you found the abandoned Mercedes."

"What?" interjected Tao. "At this time of night? I was under the impression you were headed back to the hotel."

"Yes, that was our intent." Amanda tried to sound nonchalant.

"However, I had a . . . " Amanda wondered how to phrase it so the detective would not think she was a nut to be working off her instinct again.

"A *feeling*," the detective chimed in, "or a sense that you would find something useful to the investigation?"

"Yes, I did, Detective. I hope you don't think it silly or a waste of time, but we did end up finding a piece of a cell phone memory board. It looks like it has been crushed and there was only a small piece—out of place in the middle of nowhere. And it wasn't there for long, no rust or any signs of exposure."

The detective was silent, so Amanda continued. "Also, as we were searching the area for further evidence, up the road a ways we came upon some sort of opening into the jungle, like a well-hidden path. I am not sure if you are aware that it exists, but we were about to take a look when you called."

"Ms. Bannon, I cannot begin to tell you how dangerous the jungle can be on the Big Island. This is still a relatively rural and undeveloped island." Then the detective sighed heavily, and Amanda felt a bit sorry for him. She started to think that his distrust of them was misplaced contempt for society—how hard he worked for such little reward. *His line of work must be very stressful and no longer fulfilling*, she thought. "Well, I guess you are not going to change your mind. Let me just explain that you are putting yourself and your husband at risk. The jungle is not safe, and should something happen to you my men would not be willing to search until there was some light to work with. Getting a search helicopter out at this time of night would take hours and require endless amounts of paperwork."

"What are you saying, Detective?" Amanda wondered if the detective was feeling OK. *Perhaps a long vacation would help.*

"I am saying, go at your own risk. You will lose cellular coverage, but I am sure you have some provisions with you. I hope I will not be looking for five bodies tomorrow morning." Then silence, and Amanda realized the detective had hung up.

"What was that all about?" Jake inquired. "Didn't sound like you were ordering pizza, although I could use a Rea's house special with sausage right now." Amanda was amused at the reference to their favorite Italian restaurant back home in Calgary. Rea's used to be called Sandro until a fire gutted the place. The owners took the opportunity to rebuild it into a fantastic little hole in the wall, a well-regarded restaurant. It was always full, but the family, whom the Bannons knew well, always had a table for them. Their thin-crust pizza had the most amazing sauce and fresh toppings that made her mouth water just thinking about it. Jake and Amanda could lose an entire afternoon there, drinking Ripassa and talking. Jake interrupted Amanda's thoughts. "Well, are we gonna stand here all night or are you gonna fill me in so we can start our trek of doom?"

"Oh, yeah, just fantasizing about Rea's pizza. Sorry. Well, it was Detective Tao, and he was acting funny—not funny ha ha but funny strange. He kind of gave us his blessing to go get our asses handed to us in the jungle. Cool, huh?"

Jake looked quizzically at Amanda. "Well, that *is* interesting, but what pisses me off is that you got a signal out here on your cell phone. I knew I shouldn't have changed over to 4G. What a bunch of crap. I get a signal when I am standing right on top of one of their towers, but otherwise . . ."

"Well, technically, your phone should be backward compatible; I think it's end-user error, dear," Amanda said, grinning. "That is why I never jump on the first new thing that comes out. There is something to be said for tried-and-true technology. Now, let's get going. We are running out of time, and I think the detective intends to give us this one free pass only."

Jake nodded and bent down so Amanda could apply the black makeup on his face and arms. Jake did the same for Amanda, then they holstered their pieces, grabbed their packs, and set out through the secret entrance into the blackness beyond.

CHAPTER 18

BERNIE WRIGHT PACED BACK AND FORTH. It was past midnight, but he couldn't sleep a wink. All he could think about was Taylor and Gail. He knew that they were both tough girls, but as he had learned through his years in the police force, even the toughest wills can be broken, and fear can do that faster than anything else. He hoped that they could stay strong through this ordeal. He would be taking a leave of absence as soon as he could get hold of his boss.

Bernie remembered how close he was with Taylor before he and Gail split up. Taylor had been very angry for some time with both of them, but mostly with her mother. Bernie knew that Taylor wouldn't understand the real reason Gail wanted out of the relationship, and he knew Gail would never say anything to Taylor. Gail was good that way. She wanted Taylor to think the best of her father. Since Taylor was born, she had adored her father. Having a police officer for a dad made her feel protected and special. He was one of the good guys, and she could never fault him for anything. Now, Bernie frowned as he remembered the events leading up to the end of his marriage. Yes, Gail ran off with Keith, his partner of eight years on the force, but there was a reason only he and Gail knew.

He remembered going out with the gang, celebrating the retirement of a member of their team who decided to call it quits at fifty-five. "Freedom 55" was the theme for the evening. There were a lot of stories and hours of singing and drinking. Bernie hadn't been that drunk since his academy days. That night he was introduced to a very young, beautiful Spanish rookie named Margarite Romero. He was quite taken with her, and she seemed very interested in his steady stream of stories about his experiences over the years with his now-retired partner, Jonesy. Gail was no longer interested in hearing those stories. When Taylor was born, Gail stopped paying attention to him, and he understood that sometimes that happens when a child is introduced into a relationship. But it never changed back. He continued to adore Gail, but she seemed almost bored with him. He didn't understand why. He hadn't changed much over the years. He kept himself in good physical condition. She had to understand that his job was stressful, and she had to give some concession to the situation. He was tired of being treated second rate in their relationship. He felt he was no longer important in her life.

Later that evening he offered to share a cab with Margarite, since she lived in Inglewood and he was in the northwest part of town. "But that's not even close. In fact, it's the opposite way from my condo," she chided him as she took his arm.

"I just want to make sure you get home safe. I am an officer of the law. To serve and protect is my forte." His words were slightly slurred.

"OK then," she said with a brilliant white smile. "Only if you let me pay the fare, at least to my house. I insist."

With that the two of them jumped into a yellow cab for the fifteen-minute ride from downtown to Inglewood. Sitting in the back of the cab, Bernie could feel the heat rising between them. Margarite moved her leg closer to Bernie's, and they were now lightly touching. She was wearing a very short skirt, exposing much of her muscular legs. Bernie had to force his eyes away several times. As they got closer to Margarite's condo, she asked if he would like to come in for a nightcap. Bernie started to say no when Margarite moved her leg over, on top of his, forcing her skirt to slide up just a little bit higher. Bernie couldn't help but look over and then up at her face. She slowly licked her full, red lips, and he could feel his heart beating hard in his chest as his erection started to become noticeable. "One drink won't hurt, I guess, but I can only stay for one. It's getting late."

Bernie ended up paying the cab driver, as he felt obligated at this point.

Just seeing Margarite's thigh made him feel like he had something to pay for. A feeling of guilt started to slowly creep up from deep within him, but Margarite now slid her hand in his and led him up the stairs to her front door. The apartment was dimly lit, but Bernie could see that Margarite had not only good but expensive taste. Hanging on the wall were some fine pieces of art, and beautiful sculptures decorated the side tables. The floor was hardwood—real hardwood, not that click-in type you could buy at Home Depot. The couch was a nice Italian leather, the kind that feels like butter on your skin. She looked over at Bernie with a flirty smile. "Would you like a beer or a glass of red wine? I have a 2005 Sassicaia I opened earlier, so it should be pleasant."

"Sure." Bernie had managed to learn a little bit about wines from hanging out with his friends the Bannons. They had introduced a few good Italian wines to his collection—not that his collection was of any real quality, like the Bannon's, but he had two bottles of Sassicaia and a few bottles of Tignanello in his small wine fridge.

She walked in with two Riedel wine glasses half full and sat down on the couch. "I guess you are wondering how I can afford all of this?" She looked like a goddess with golden skin against the cream-colored Italian leather. He sat down, and she handed him a glass. "My parents . . . *Salute.*" She held up her glass, and he clinked it. She never took her eyes off his face as she drank deeply from the glass. "Oh, there is nothing better than a full-bodied glass of red, don't you agree?" Bernie nodded. He didn't trust opening his mouth to speak, so he took a gulp of the wine, a far bigger gulp than he wanted to, but thank goodness for the smooth finish of the wine. He was able to swallow it before he realized that Margarite had undone her blouse. Not all the way, just enough to show her ample breasts, pushed up in a very sexy, lacy bra, the kind you find at Victoria's Secret, not La Senza.

"Hey," he sputtered, "I don't think this is such a good idea. We both have to work on the force together. You're new and, well, I'm old."

Margarite could sense that things were not moving the way she had planned, so she moved closer to Bernie on the couch and leaned down to place her glass on the coffee table. When she did this her blouse hung open more and Bernie could see her fine tight abdomen down to the top of her skirt. He felt the blood flow increase between his legs and tried to think of icebergs in the Atlantic to calm himself down. She then sat back up and placed her hand on his arm. "Bernie, is this the way you are going to treat your new trainee?"

Shock registered on Bernie's face at first, and then he stammered, "Oh, they told me I was getting a rookie to train up, but I didn't know who it was."

"Surprise," she said in a sultry voice. "Don't you think this could be fun?"

"Well, I think we should think about how this, may affect us professionally," he said, trying to remain calm and confident in his tone.

"I think I can be extremely professional. How about you? Do you think you can handle the heat or do you need to get out of the kitchen?" With this she slid her hand down his arm, over his leg, and then placed it firmly over his member. She could feel it grow under her touch.

With that Bernie was lost. He couldn't think. All the booze had made him giddy, and all he could think about was the hard, burning piece of him that was now out of control. He closed his eyes to try to make the feeling subside. He tried to remember the last time he had felt this kind of rush with Gail, and he couldn't. He opened his eyes wide when he felt Margarite pull his penis out of his pants. He was frozen in ecstasy as she slid her lusty lips over his member. Her wet mouth worked its way up and down, and he was past the point of no return. This was an amazing feeling, one he had not felt since his college days with Gail. He had not had a blow job since before Taylor was born. Bernie was amazed at how adept Margarite was at sucking him. Obviously, this wasn't her first rodeo. Soon she was sliding all the way down, taking all of him. Bernie was not huge, but he was a good six inches and thick, so he was frankly impressed with this young lady. She must have had him halfway down her throat, and he didn't care. *Choke on it*, was all he could think. *Take it all, baby; you want it, take it.* She stopped for a moment to lick her lips. Then she pulled his pants off. She tore her shirt off and moved between his legs to work his piece with more vigor. He bent forward and unclipped her bra. She straightened up and placed his penis between her D-cup breasts. The soft flesh against his member was intense.

She stopped and began licking his balls, stroking her tongue up his shaft. She put it back in her mouth and continued to work her magic, faster and faster until he came in a gush that seemed like he had been storing it forever. She had no problem swallowing everything, again impressive.

After that night the two of them worked late most nights. His favorite was having her blow him in her uniform in the back of his car out on Highway 1A, near the Indian reservation. She had kept quiet about the whole thing, right up until it was time for her first review.

Bernie knew he wouldn't be able to recommend her for a promotion. She had been OK on her trials and tests, but he knew she needed more experience. Her reports were crap, lacking the proper time and details. He had mentioned to Margarite on a regular basis that he could not give her a recommendation without seeing improvement. She would just smile and say things like, "Well, your cock has seen lots of improvements, hasn't it?"

The nightmare started one morning while they were out on a training patrol. Margarite demanded, "I think you should put in a recommendation for me to be promoted."

"You're not ready," he calmly stated. "It's dangerous for us to put you out there when you are not ready to pass all the aptitude exams, and in your last shooting drill, you shot two innocent people."

"You have the authority to override that, don't you?"

"Yes, but that wouldn't be right," he said with a sigh.

"Tell me, Bernie, is what you and I are doing considered right? If so, why don't you call your wife and tell her all the *right* things you are doing?" Her voice was like venom being injected directly into Bernie's heart.

"When we started this, you said you would remain professional about it." Even while saying this, Bernie knew it sounded weak. He knew that someone like her would never do the things she was doing to him without a reason. He had known all along, and a deep shame came over him.

"Bernie, it's your call: either you give the recommendation or I call Gail. The choice is yours." She got out of the car and strolled over to the Starbucks across the street. Right then Bernie knew what he had to do. He pulled out his cell phone and called Gail.

CHAPTER 19

GAIL HAD BEEN INCONSOLABLE. She knew things weren't perfect at home, but she never imagined he would do that to her. She went into survival mode. Right from the beginning she wanted to shield Taylor from the truth about her father. She never told her exactly what happened but said that she was depressed because he had to work so much. She stopped eating and grew thin. Taylor was worried sick about her. They had first told Taylor that her mom was going through a depression, but after a while they knew that Taylor could see it was something else. They decided to tell her that they were having some issues and that they were going to get help as a family.

Gail and Bernie went to counseling together to try to save their marriage, if for no other reason than Taylor's sake. Bernie realized he was just as much at fault for their diminishing sex life. He learned that he couldn't expect his wife to be ready and waiting for him each night after a tough day's work. He discovered that women need some kind of passion that starts right from the time they get up in the morning to get them in the mood. He came to realize it took extra work to woo his wife and keep her interested. Bernie wished he would have known all these things before he went ahead and ruined his marriage for good. The counseling helped Gail get hold of her anger and hurt. It gave her an outlet to vent and be heard. But it didn't change her decision in the end. She just couldn't deal with the fact that her husband, the only man she had ever been with, could do this to her. She said it wasn't fair to Bernie or Taylor that she lived a lie, because she felt she could never trust Bernie again. That hurt Bernie more than anything else.

Gail asked Bernie to move out, and the two of them explained to Taylor that her mom just needed some time for herself. That may have been a mistake, as it perhaps gave Taylor the indication that there might be a reconciliation and that her dad might eventually come home to live with them again. Of course, that wasn't the case.

Bernie found himself a one-bedroom apartment in the northeast end of town, close to Taylor and Gail, so he could continue to be a regular part of Taylor's life. Often he would come by early and drive her to school or take her out for dinner and a movie. He immersed himself in spending time with his daughter, hoping that Gail would one day forgive him and they could be a family again.

In the meantime, things with Margarite were getting progressively worse. Although he thought by calling her bluff and confessing to Gail about the affair he would force her to back off, instead she seemed to snap. She claimed that she was going to file a sexual harassment case against him and that he would be kicked off the force for good. Things couldn't be any worse for him, or so he thought.

One night he was taking Taylor home and recognized his ex-partner's car in the driveway. Keith Stevens had been Bernie's partner long before Bernie was assigned to train the rookie. They had gotten pretty close over the years, and Bernie had confided in him months earlier about what was going on. He had told Keith that he planned to end it with Margarite. Keith, who had been single all his life, had told Bernie that he was brain-dead if he didn't understand what a great catch he had in Gail. Bernie didn't disagree with Keith, but at the time he was not thinking with the right head.

Bernie asked Taylor why Keith was there and Taylor shot back, "He's always here. Sometimes he helps Mom bring home groceries. Other times he just pops in to say hi and see if she needs anything fixed. They just sit at the kitchen table and talk a lot."

"Oh," was all Bernie could manage. A month or so later, Bernie received a notice from a downtown law firm. Gail had filed for divorce. Bernie's heart sank. He called in sick the next day and sat in front of the TV with a bottle of scotch and a bag of Doritos. He did not move for hours. The phone rang on several occasions, but he did not answer. He was contemplating how he would go on without Gail, or if he even wanted to go on. Then his cell phone rang. Taylor's face lit up the screen. It was late, so he answered in case something was wrong.

"Daddy?" Her voice sounded so tiny, so small and fragile.

"Yes, sweetie." He tried hard not to slur his words, the eighteen-year-old Macallan feeling like it was trying to come back up his esophagus.

"Where are you? I tried you at work and at your apartment. Are you OK?"

"Yeah." Bernie tried to put some energy into his tone, but it wasn't coming off as well as he wanted. "Well, I'm feeling a bit sick, so I took the day off. I think I may have the flu or something."

"OK, 'cause I thought you and I were going to go shopping today. You never called or came by."

Oh shit, Bernie thought, *is it Saturday already?* "Oh, sorry, sweetie. With me being sick and all, I totally forgot. Can I make it up to you? How about next weekend?"

"Umm, OK, but we have to go early 'cause I have a band concert Friday night. Remember? Hope you are coming."

"I wouldn't miss it for the world." With that he said good night and realized he did have something to live for. His daughter needed him, and he wasn't going to lose his wife *and* his daughter.

He thought about calling Margarite and decided against it. Things had quieted down with her. After all the threats she made, he found out that he wasn't the only one on the force that she was "using." Apparently she had a real problem. Although she had put in a complaint, it was one of several and was buried, under review.

The following week Bernie got himself together and headed into work. His chief called him into his office. "Yes, sir, you wanted to see me?"

"Yeah, Bernie, listen, Keith Stevens has taken a transfer into another unit. He wanted to tell you himself, but you were away last Friday. He took up his new post today, so I told him I would let you know. Listen, I know you guys have been partners for what, eight years now? And it will be hard to switch but . . . " the lieutenant's voice trailed off as Bernie started putting two and two together.

He thanked the lieutenant and said, "OK, change is good." He walked back to his station, grabbed his cell phone, and went outside, where nobody else could hear his conversation. Gail answered on the first ring.

"How long have you and my partner been fucking?" Bernie's voice was heated and filled with a vengeance Gail had never heard before.

"We haven't been," Gail said. "What are you talking about?"

"Let's see, first I get a notice from your new lawyer that you are filing for divorce, and the next thing I know Keith has transferred out of my unit and I am getting a new partner. So what I want to know is how long the two of you had been fucking before you decided to take action."

"Well, first of all, we weren't *fucking* at all. If you recall, you were the one doing the fucking." Bernie's cheeks burned as he realized that she was right. "Keith started coming over to offer support after your *indiscretions* were made known to me. We've become close, but he has never laid a hand on me. He's been a perfect gentleman, more than I can say for you." Again Bernie felt the sting of the insult but knew that he had nothing, absolutely nothing, he could say. He was the dog, not Keith. Why would Keith want to continue being his partner? Gail was right.

"I'm sorry," he said. "It's just all been such a shock to me. I guess I kept thinking that somehow, someway I could get you back, get you to trust me and love me again."

"I never stopped loving you, Bernie. I just stopped liking you. I can't be with someone I don't like. Don't get upset with Keith. He has been a pillar of strength for me. He has helped me realize that I am worth something."

"Gail, you are a beautiful, wonderful woman. Of course you are worth something. To me you are worth everything." Bernie had to work hard at not breaking down right there outside the RCMP station.

"Well, you sure have a funny way of treating someone that is worth everything to you. Anyway, if you must know, Keith and I *have* started seeing each other. Like I said, nothing has happened, though. I want to make sure Taylor is OK with it first, but you should know, 'cause he may become more of a permanent figure around the house."

"Keith has never been married," Bernie spat out. "He has no experience taking care of a family. He lives a single man's life; he picks up chicks wherever he can, claiming all the good ones are taken."

"What are you saying, Bernie?" Gail was now on the verge of tears. "That a single man won't trade his life with other women to be with me? From my seat, it doesn't seem to matter whether a man is single or married, but I am not going to spend the rest of my life alone and unhappy because you decided that's what I should do. You no longer have a right to discuss my life and how I live it. If I were you, I would be more concerned with yourself and your daughter. Hopefully, you can be there for her and do the right thing by her. Perhaps that way you can regain some of your ethical self," she blurted out before hanging up.

Bernie knew Gail was right. He knew he had to focus now on Taylor and making sure she was OK through it all. He knew Taylor would be very unhappy about the divorce that was about to happen. *Maybe*, he thought, *Taylor could help change Gail's mind*. He didn't think so, but the thought stayed with him.

CHAPTER 20

TAYLOR SHIVERED, NOT SO MUCH BECAUSE OF THE COOL ROOM, BUT MORE AT THE THOUGHT OF THAT MONSTER COMING BACK. She was now more thirsty than hungry and thought of all those things she had read stating that humans could survive a long while without food but only days without water. Her eyes scanned the dark room again. She had not moved from her little spot in the moonlit area near the window for hours. She felt safer in the light, but she had to pee. She crawled on all fours toward where the shape of the bucket was. She pulled down her shorts and panties and went in the bucket, shaking her backside to keep as clean as possible. Just as she pulled her shorts up, she heard the lock in the door rattle and scrambled back to her dimly lit space on the floor.

Taylor's eyes grew wide as the door opened. She expected the horrible face of the snake man, but instead a smaller figure in a black, hooded robe swiftly moved inside and placed what seemed to be a flask and a bundled-up cloth on the dirt floor. She couldn't see his face as he glided back to the door, shut it, and turned the lock. Taylor slowly moved closer to the door. She picked up the flask and shook it. She could hear the swish of liquid. She greedily pulled out the rubber stopper. *What if this is poison?* she thought. *Under the circumstances it would be a good way to go.* It had been days since they were kidnapped. Her dad was not coming. The police were not coming. Nobody was coming. She took a big, long drink. The water was tepid, but she was grateful. It was the best-tasting water she had ever had in her life. She stopped herself from guzzling the entire flask. *Who knows when they'll bring me more water. Besides, peeing in that bucket is not all that much fun.*

She looked over at the little cloth bundle. It was tied with a piece of string. She untied it and opened the cloth. There was a piece of bread and something that looked like beef jerky. She had always been a picky eater, but she was so famished she didn't care what it was. She ripped a piece of the jerky off with her teeth and chewed it with gusto. As she chewed, savoring the flavor, she wondered, *Why did they wait so long to feed me? What is this all about?*

She started to go over the facts again as she knew them. Carlos had promised her that if she came to Hawaii two things would happen: she would be with him, and he would break up her mom and Keith's relationship. He was going to show her how it could be done using the magic arts they had been studying. He told her that she was the pure one, the goddess who would make all this happen. She recalled how much she loved being called a goddess, but she didn't feel much like a goddess now—hungry, tired, scared, and wondering what had become of her mom and Keith. This was not how Carlos had explained that it would work. At least it was not how she had interpreted what he said. *Maybe Carlos had nothing to do with all this*, she thought. *Maybe he was getting help from someone else, who then decided to turn on him. That's what it must be*, she tried to convince herself. *It just doesn't seem to make sense. Carlos told me a car would be waiting and that everything else would then fall into place. He didn't tell me I'd be drugged and thrown into a dungeon and separated from my mother—never mind fuckface with the snakes carved into his head. Nope, Carlos is either part of all this or he is dead.* Either way, she didn't care. She hated him.

CHAPTER 21

"Amanda, did you hear that?" Jake whispered loudly. He thought he was being quiet, but it still sounded like he was talking at full volume because the rain forest had become still and silent.

"All I hear is you—amplified, in fact."

"Shush." Jake put his finger to his lips, then pointed two fingers to his eyes and out toward the right. Amanda stared directly into the darkness and tried to focus. She closed her eyes for five seconds to let them grow accustomed to the blackness. When she reopened them, she would notice any shadows, but there was nothing.

"Jake, I don't think there's anything out there. I would have felt it before you heard it." Amanda looked over to see Jake snickering under his makeup.

"What the hell?" She glared at him.

"OK, OK, honestly I have just always wanted to do that eye-pointing thing you see in the Navy SEAL movies." He grinned so wide that Amanda had to smile.

"Come on, fool." She moved forward slowly. It was clear some kind of path had been cut out before them, and her senses were telling her they were on to something, hopefully the place they needed to get to for a rescue and not a burial.

Amanda heard a rustling and looked up just in time to see a snake slither down a tree and quickly venture off into the night. She was frozen with horror.

"Whoa, that was close. Thank goodness it was just a baby. I bet its mama is around eight to ten feet," Jake exaggerated. He knew that the brown tree snake, the only kind found on the island, was harmless. It was his attempt to shake Amanda out of her semifrozen state. Amanda had a huge fear of snakes. When she was in third grade, her teacher arranged for Agnes, a six-foot boa constrictor, to visit her class on a play day. The kids took turns holding Agnes, and when it was Amanda's turn, the trainer put the snake around her shoulders. The snake, perhaps being somewhat agitated from all the excitement of the day, decided it was time to have a little fun and began tightening herself around Amanda's shoulders and neck, which were some-what smaller than those of the average eight-year-old. She had turned purple and was about to pass out when they finally managed to slide the snake off of her. Ever since then she only needed to see a snake and she would be scared stiff. It was one of the few things that actually got to Amanda Bannon.

"I'm OK," she said, letting out a long, slow breath. "There are more important things to think about right now." With a nod to Jake she took the lead on the trail as usual.

"Why do you always take the lead on the trails, honey?" Jake asked.

"Because I like to see what's coming from ahead, and if anything is sneaking up behind us, it will eat you first," she said without a hint of compassion.

"Always the joker," he mumbled under his breath.

Farther ahead they could hear running water—actually, more like gush-ing water. And soon enough the dense growth opened upon a small ledge of mud that slid into a river about a hundred feet across. In the clear moonlight they could see that the path resumed on the other side, enticing them to cross the silver river. "My goodness, and I forgot my one swimsuit," Amanda mused. "The water is rushing pretty fast." Amanda knew if she was going to bungle things up anywhere it would be here. Even during the dry season, when there wasn't such a strong current, it would be difficult for her to cross. The river didn't seem to be too deep, but she was also only five foot four, so she knew the slightest hole could put her under. Jake was a strong swimmer, so he could cross first. He pulled out the lightweight, fifty-foot Mammut Matterhorn rope. It was durable enough for climbing and tied nicely when you happened to run into a river or two. He tied the rope around Amanda's waste and clipped it to her pants, then let about eight feet of rope go and did the same to himself. The backpacks were waterproof and had built-in buoyancy-control devices. They were experimental; Jake was testing them for a friend's firm. He tied one end of the rope around their backpacks and carried the other end as he trekked out ahead, and Amanda followed, trying to keep her balance and jamming her boots in between rocks on the riverbed to gain some control. They were nearly halfway across, with the water rushing past furiously, threatening to take them for a ride, when—*whoosh!*—Jake suddenly disappeared underwater, and before Amanda could figure out what had happened, she was dragged by the waist with just enough time to gulp one last breath before going down into the dark river after Jake.

CHAPTER 22

"HAS THE GIRL BEEN FED?" Carlos asked his companion. The hooded figure nodded and turned to walk away. "Wait, are the parents still alive?" The sentry stopped, nodded without turning around, and then continued to walk down the slope.

Good, Carlos thought, *Liag wants everyone alive, at least until he arrives. How long now? It has been three nights, so he will be here on the fifth night: Sunday, January 2.* That gave them plenty of time to get everything prepared for the seventh night, when together they would pour the blood of the virgin girl over the altar in the first part of the ritual that would end with Carlos sacrificing himself. Then, he would join the souls that waited for him to lead him to utopia.

It was time to make contact with Liag, time to set things in motion. He pulled out the Iridium satellite phone, found a clear spot to get the line of sight to the device, and dialed Liag's private number. The phone rang twice before Liag answered.

"Yes," was all he said.

"It is time." Carlos motioned with his free hand although nobody was there to see him. "Liag, it is time. You must come soon. I have started the preparations for the sacrifice; we cannot be late."

"Yes, yes," Liag said in a calm, soothing voice. "Do not concern yourself, my son. We will ensure that the timing is not jeopardized. Is the girl hurt?"

"No." Carlos smiled. "I have kept her pure."

"Good." Liag was stern. "We cannot have her harmed in any way prior to the ritual. What of the man and the woman?"

"Alive," was all Carlos said.

"I want them alive. I want them to witness the sacrifice. I want them to know the truth. Then I want the man to die in front of the woman. These are the lessons we must instill in these people. Think of your childhood. Think, Carlos. Who was there for you? Who protected you?" Carlos's eyes filled with tears, but he did not let them fall. He suddenly felt the hatred for this world, the hatred for all men and women who sat back in their lazy, self-absorbed vessels and did nothing while others suffered. He hated those who watched all the atrocities on the news and then turned the TV off and sat down with their families to have a nice dinner without another thought. He hated that there were people enjoying comfortable lives while others—the starving, the beaten, and the broken—were condemned to a life of hurt due to nothing more than circumstance. His rage could not be contained. He put both arms up toward the sky and roared into the night.

On the other end of the satellite phone, Liag heard a bloodcurdling cry. He smiled and hung up the phone.

CHAPTER 23

ALTHOUGH IT WAS DARK, THE MOONLIGHT SHONE DIRECTLY
THROUGH TO THE BOTTOM OF THE RIVERBED. Amanda could see
Jake's figure in front of her struggling, with his right leg buried deep in what
Amanda thought might be quicksand. Jake had yanked hard on the rope to
draw the floating gear pack to him, which in turn yanked Amanda down
into the river, but she knew right away what he was trying to get hold of and
swam toward the packs. She partly deflated the packs to reduce their buoy-
ancy to take them down to Jake's level and unzipped the side pocket where
they had stored the underwater breathing devices. The devices, designed
by an Israeli diver, used the water itself to create oxygen, not air. However,
it meant there was very limited time until the apparatus would no longer
produce enough oxygen for regular breathing. The ones Amanda and Jake
had were prototypes, only lent to them on the condition of confidentiality
to allow them to test the units prior to going into full-scale beta. Because
Amanda and Jake had friends who happened to be scientists and who understood their love for diving, they were two of the first divers allowed to try
the new device, now a handheld item that only lasted about ten minutes,
due to the small filtering system.

Amanda could see Jake was getting close to his limit for holding his
breath. Jake had trained with the Navy SEALs and could hold his breath
for some time, but when someone is suddenly taken underwater without a

chance to get a good, deep breath, the time is shortened by quite a bit. She quickly stuck the device in Jake's mouth and he slowly started to breathe in, then exhale through his nose. He too knew the limited time they had to work with and, with eyes wide, gestured toward his stuck leg. Amanda, though first thinking this must be some kind of quicksand, surmised that it couldn't be, due to the fact that quicksand is easily liquefied when water is mixed in with it. If this was quicksand, it would be very easy to get out of. *It must be a small mud hole*, thought Amanda. She tried to pry Jake's leg out while he twisted, but to no avail. She was keenly aware that they had about seven minutes before the filtering system on the breathing apparatus would start to slow down. She went back up and into her pack and removed a hunting knife. Jake's eyes went wide again, and she smiled, conveying that her intentions were not to cut his leg off. She dug quickly around the mud hole, wishing she had packed her diving knife instead, but who knew they would end up underwater in the jungle? The diving knife had a better grip and release for underwater functionality. She was making progress around the claylike mud, but it was slow. She could feel a slight panic in her gut as the minutes ticked by and her internal clock sounded a silent alarm. After about five minutes of digging, she could feel the heel of Jake's boot and could tell that the mud was especially liking the leather and did not want to let go. So she dug away at the front of the boot, diligently trying not to cut too deep but accidentally sliding the knife down into Jake's foot. When the front was mostly clear, she cut through the laces. She could tell that the breathing device was now producing about half the oxygen it was previously allowing, and her breathing became shallow to accommodate; she knew Jake would be doing the same. She had cut though most of the laces by the time the device gave out. She held her last bit of oxygen and was getting the euphoric feeling that she knew came with breathing oxygen instead of air, but because they were at a shallow depth she knew it was not dangerous. She could see that no air bubbles were coming from Jake, either, and tried to help him remove his foot from the boot. Sliding it out seemed to take an eternity, and she felt a dizzy sensation from holding her breath. Jake knew she could not hold her breath for much longer and struggled and pulled at his leg with both arms—with nothing to brace himself on or push off from with his other leg, it was nearly impossible. Jake was tapping Amanda on the shoulder and pointed up toward the surface of the river. She nodded her understanding and left his foot, swam up, broke the surface, took three huge gasps of air, and shot back down to Jake. She then placed her lips over his and breathed the air into his lungs. She went back up and took one large breath for herself and headed back down. Just when she was ready to go back up, she felt his foot give way and slide at an awkward angle up and out of the boot. She headed straight to the packs, pumped the air pressure back up, and they both broke the surface of the water gasping and coughing for several seconds before they could even speak.

"I told you to get size ten wide," Amanda said between gasps for air, and Jake smiled, a pained look on his face. She could tell he had severely twisted, or perhaps broken, his ankle to get out of the boot. They headed for shore, swimming slowly and reaching the other side. Amanda helped pull the packs and Jake onto the shore. They lay there for several minutes, looking up at the star-filled sky, listening to the quiet rush of the river when suddenly they heard in the distance a bloodcurdling cry. It was definitely human.

CHAPTER 24

THE HELICOPTER WAS A BELL 206 JETRANGER, MANUFACTURED BY BELL HELICOPTER AT ITS MIRABEL PLANT IN QUEBEC. It was originally built for the U.S. Army's Light Observation Program, and when it was not selected, Bell redesigned the airframe and successfully marketed it for both commercial and private use.

Liag was tired. He piloted the helicopter from Maui, where he had been when he talked to Carlos. He was ready to go and wanted to ensure that Carlos was ready to receive him, that everything was going according to plan. It took a little more than forty-five minutes to fly to the Big Island in the Bell. He gave little thought to the complicated handling of the JetRanger as his mind was fully occupied with the plans he had for the captives. Carlos had done his work, but now it was time for Liag to take the reins. He had waited diligently, putting together all the pieces so that he would finally get revenge and have peace. Carlos was just the instrument he would use to deal the final blow.

Liag thought back to when he met Carlos. He remembered how easy it was to convince the young man of the plan. He acted like a father to Carlos, the father he never had. At first Carlos did not respond, did not believe. He had been not only physically abused, but he had been mentally abused as well. He was disengaged from understanding human compassion. It took several visits on a regular basis to finally get Carlos even to acknowledge his presence, and trust only came after months of cultivating the relationship. Where the two finally connected was on the topic of religion, and mostly black religion. Carlos began to believe that he could have purpose, and Liag encouraged him, showing him how all his sufferings of the past were meant to be. They were the tests to strengthen Carlos in the final hours to fulfill the plan, the final relief of the burden he had carried for so many years. A smile played upon Liag's face as he remembered the Carlos then and the Carlos now, a devoted disciple ready to give his life and ready to take the lives of others in order to see them through the final steps of their plan.

Liag maneuvered the aircraft very low over the hills and mountainous areas of the Big Island and crested the large ridge where he saw the lighted area and landing space. It was quite amazing how little space the Bell required to land, and the clearing was well hidden. Unless you actually knew it was there, you would miss it completely. He had taken months preparing the area, and as he slowly came into the clearing he could see the well-built structures, the little round holes that were the windows of the cavern-style huts now used to house the captives. Eight red marker lights formed a circle where he was to land. As he brought the JetRanger down in a smooth arc, he saw a large robed figure holding a flickering torch. It was Carlos. A hulking presence even from a distance, he seemed as ominous as the Devil himself.

CHAPTER 25

THE THUD-THUD-THUDDING OF A HELICOPTER BROKE INTO TAY-
LOR'S DISMAL DREAM. Large, revolting snakes were chasing her. She was
running but couldn't get away. They began swirling all around her and then
were slithering all over a face, the man's face she had seen earlier that evening. In her dream she screamed for her father to come and help her. She
screamed until her head began to thud-thud-thud. She slowly opened her
eyes and was in a daze. She suddenly recognized the thudding as the sound
of a helicopter close by. Taylor sat up straight. Could it be? Was it a rescue?
Her heart started to beat hard in her chest as she hoped with all her might
that it was the local police or the FBI or whoever took care of kidnappings
in the states. Perhaps it was her dad. Could it be? He flew the helicopters
for RCMP chases now and then when he wasn't working behind a desk.
The helicopter motor started to slow down, and after a few minutes it was
shut off. She listened intently, expecting to hear shouting or even shooting,
but it was deathly silent. She waited and waited. The longer she waited, the
more her hopes were diminished. She closed her eyes to rest but tried not to
fall asleep for fear of falling back into the same nightmare. After a while she
started to believe she had only imagined the sound of the helicopter, that it
was just part of her dream and that she had still been in the haze between
sleep and wakefulness when she thought she heard the engine spool down.

I need to stand, she told herself. *If there is a chance to escape, I need to be ready.* Taylor tried to stand, but her legs were like Jell-O. After three days in the dank hole with hardly any food or water, or exercise, she was very weak. She used the wall of her cell to support herself as she slid up. *Why haven't they rescued us? Where are we that nobody can find us? Where is my dad?* she thought in anguish as hot tears streamed down her face. She reverted to being a scared little child.

CHAPTER 26

THEY HAD BEEN IN THE JUNGLE FOR NEARLY FOUR HOURS, AND IT WAS GETTING CLOSE TO MIDNIGHT. The moon still shone brilliantly, lighting up the path before them that still showed the hidden way if you looked closely. The cry they heard piercing the otherwise quiet night was frightful, but in a way it was gratifying to know that they were at least on the right track and Amanda's suspicions and feelings were confirmed. It would be such a waste to find that they were going the wrong way, but again that never seemed to happen when Amanda used her sixth sense. It unnerved Jake that they were not using a logical method to track the missing people, and yet he knew that she would lead them to the journey's end. What he didn't want to know was what was at the end of the journey.

Jake's ankle throbbed while Amanda wrapped it in tensor bandage, and he groaned. "Suck it up, buttercup," Amanda said with a slight grin. "I'm sorry it hurts, buddy, but at least you didn't break it. What good would you be then, huh?" Jake's unhappy look convinced Amanda to take a softer approach. Jake was not someone who whined, but in this case she felt he had a right.

"OK, you're right. If you weren't out here on this wild goose chase with me your ankle would be fine and we would be having a great steak and a bottle of Cheval Blanc somewhere in Honolulu right now." Amanda referenced their favorite red wine from the Bordeaux region in France. "I know this is not the New Year's you were planning, but I also know you are just as concerned about helping Taylor and Gail as I am."

Jake nodded while gritting his teeth. Amanda dug through the pack and asked, "Demerol or Tylenol 3?"

"Have any Advil gel caps?" Jake responded. He knew Amanda always carried those. "Still afraid of prescription drugs, huh? You won't get addicted, Jake. You're made differently."

"I can tough it out. No worries, but an Advil will help, and those gel caps are fast." Amanda pulled out a couple of Advils from her baggie full of medication. She always had an assortment of meds, just in case. Jake swallowed two with a bit of the water from their canister, which they were preserving carefully. They didn't know how long this adventure would last. They both hoped it would be done before morning, but it wasn't looking that way. Amanda was also wondering if they would ever see the end of this night. It seemed like it was dragging on forever.

"Jake, do you want to try standing?" Amanda had untied them from the packs and was wrapping the rope up in an easy eight configuration. "Sure, let's see what happens." Jake slowly raised himself off the ground using his good leg and gently placed his sore ankle on the ground. Then he put some weight on the ankle. "Not too bad. Nice job on the bandage. Good support."

"Try walking."

Jake gingerly took a few steps and grimaced. "Not so good," he said between clenched teeth.

"Give it a few, and the Advil will kick in." Amanda busied herself putting away the items they had used during their river adventure and then pulled out a Clif Bar. She took a few bites and passed it over to Jake, who swallowed the rest.

"Hungry?" she asked.

"Oh, just a bit. You got me going with that comment about the steak and Cheval Blanc. What I would give . . ." He rolled his eyes heavenward and then gestured toward the jungle trail. "Let's get moving. The night is better cover for us. I don't want to still be doing this in the hot sun."

Amanda knew Jake was right. They would make better progress at night, even with his sore ankle, than when their energy was sucked out of them on a sweltering eighty-five-degree day.

CHAPTER 27

GAIL'S EYES WERE SWOLLEN FROM HER CONTINUOUS STREAM OF TEARS AND LACK OF SLEEP. She looked over at Keith, who slumbered solidly like he was at home in his own bed. All she could think about was Taylor. Where was she? Was she OK? She could only imagine how scared her little girl must be. Gail couldn't bear the thought that something had happened to Taylor. She would lose her mind. *No, she must be alive*, she thought for the hundredth time. *They wouldn't have kept us alive if she were dead. What could these people want? What was this all about?*

Gail couldn't help her stream of thoughts, which were going around in a circle as she kept trying to figure things out. Keith was no help, and she was starting to believe she had made a big mistake by being with him. Unfortunately, Bernie was right about Keith. He was selfish and inconsiderate. He didn't know much about taking care of a family. *But at least he hasn't cheated on me*, she reasoned. Even though he had violated her trust, she would have loved to see Bernie right then.

Bernie must be looking for us by now, if for no other reason than for Taylor's sake, she thought. *I know he will do everything in his power to help us, but will that be enough? The Hawaiian authorities must know we are missing. But why are we being held captive? There must be a reason: ransom or some other reason.* It was the other reason that terrified Gail.

Ever since she woke up in the dungeon Gail had spent every second going over the details of the trip. Keith thought she was crazy for playing it over and over in her mind. She thought he was insensitive for not helping her understand. She could not figure out why anyone would want to kidnap them. They had no money. They were not politically or religiously connected. Perhaps some overzealous fanatical group thought they were worth more than they were. She held on to the hope that someone, anyone, was out there doing something to try to help them.

CHAPTER 28

THEY HAD BEEN TREKKING THROUGH THE JUNGLE AT QUITE A GOOD
PACE, CONSIDERING JAKE'S ANKLE, WHEN ALL OF A SUDDEN AMANDA
STOPPED AND PUT UP HER HAND AND POINTED TO HER EAR. Jake
stood motionless, intently listening for anything unusual. Then he heard it
too. First very faint and then louder, he could make out the clear and distinct sound of a rotary blade cutting through the night sky. It was not only
loud but quite close. Although they could not see it, they knew it couldn't
have been more than a mile away. Then it moved in the direction they were
heading. *Another sign that we're on the right track*, Jake thought. He doubted
very much that Big Island Helicopters was giving a tour anywhere around
there at that time of night. He wished that it were Big Island Helicopters
giving a late-night tour, but he knew better. After the noise of the chopper
faded, Amanda turned to Jake. "What do you make of that?"

"Sounded like a single engine out here. I am going to guess either a Bell
206 Hughes 500 or an EC 130. Didn't sound like twin engines or Fenstrom
tail rotor. The pitch was off. Doubt it's a Dauphin coast guard, and it's definitely not military. Although you never know; it's tough to decipher from
this far away. Definitely not a piston engine, though, so it's not a Robinson.
It's a Bell 206 or LongRanger."

"That you know even that much is freaky," Amanda teased. "The good
news is, now we have a way out of this place. Come on, let's go."

"Well, you are assuming that whoever is flying that helicopter is associated with the kidnappers and also that they are going to the same place we're headed."

Amanda didn't even stop or look up; she just kept walking and, with all the confidence in the world, said, "No assumptions, Jake. This one I know."

Jake sighed and continued to follow Amanda. He knew she was right, and he knew this was going to get way more dangerous than either of them wanted to admit. He felt for the Glock G20 in his belt and at first was startled when it wasn't there. Then he remembered they had put the guns in the waterproof packs before crossing the river. He would remind Amanda at their next stop that the guns were better placed somewhere they could get to them quickly, although he hoped with all his might they wouldn't have to use them at all.

CHAPTER 29

THE CLOCK NEXT TO HIS BED GLOWED 11:45 P.M. Detective Tao stared at it with an uneasy feeling. The last conversation he'd had with Amanda Bannon rang in his ears, and he wondered if he should have done more to stop them. *No*, he thought, *they were determined to go on their quest no matter what I threatened.* He knew this was not their first undertaking of this sort. "They know what they are doing," he said, not realizing he had spoken out loud until his wife murmured a sleepy response: "*Who* knows what they are doing, Ron?"

He bent down and gave her a soft kiss on the forehead. "Nobody, sweetheart. Go back to sleep. I have to do a little research."

The detective moved to his computer and pulled up the Bannons' profile online. Again, nothing but accolades, awards, philanthropic endeavors. *Good people*, he thought. *I wonder if there is anything to this clairvoyance of Amanda Bannon's.* He looked up Wikipedia's definition: "The term clairvoyance (from the seventeenth-century French with *clair* meaning 'clear' and *voyance* meaning 'vision') is used to refer to the ability to gain information about an object, person, location, or physical event through means other than the known human senses. It's a form of extra-sensory perception. A person said to have the ability of clairvoyance is referred to as a clairvoyant ('one who sees clearly')."

OK, so she can see clearly, he muttered. He also read that while the ability was not officially accepted by the scientific community, there had been a few cases in which ESP was used in finding missing children and murder victims. It was not an unheard-of method of assisting in crimes. He found that there were even psychic detectives. Although they were regularly praised by police personnel for their accuracy and effectiveness, they were never given credit for any information that led to solving a case. The detective thought about how much more credible scientific evidence was than intuition and how shows like *CSI* were proof.

Tao's head started to hurt. He turned off the computer and went to the medicine cabinet in the bathroom, took out two extra-strength Tylenol, and downed them with tap water from the sink. He crawled slowly back into bed, trying not to disturb his wife, who was softly snoring on her side. *Well*, he thought, *I hope Ms. Bannon's vision can show her where to go, but also where not to go*. With that he dozed off into a fitful sleep. He would be tired and irritated in the morning, waiting for her call.

CHAPTER 30

CARLOS'S LONG ROBE FLUTTERED HARD AS THE HELICOPTER TOUCHED DOWN. He could see Liag in the pilot's seat as he waited for the engine to spool down. After a couple of minutes he watched as his master turned off the various switches, shutting the helicopter down. Liag jumped out and walked over to Carlos, holding out his arms in a warm gesture. Carlos went to Liag and bent down on one knee. It looked like a priest performing a blessing on one of his subjects.

"The helicopter needs the blades tied," Liag said to Carlos. "Once you have done that, meet me in the main temple. It is important that we get everything in place for the ceremony." Carlos bowed, showing his respect and his unconditional acceptance of whatever Liag asked of him, and went to tie down the blades so that they wouldn't turn in the wind. Even though the landing area was completely sheltered by the dense brush surrounding it and the canopy of trees protecting the higher area, it was still prudent to secure the Bell 206.

While tying the propeller, Carlos thought back to when he first met Liag and how the older man had saved him, given him something to believe in again. It hadn't taken the authorities long to connect him to his father's death. The minister who had sat with Carlos in the field told the police about the murdered man's rage, and the old man who had taken Carlos to the hospital told them about his condition. The nurses at the hospital explained to the authorities that Carlos acted strange, like a caged animal, before he escaped in the night. It didn't take long for the police to track his whereabouts and put him in juvenile detention. Although he was still a minor, due to the severity of the crime he was tried in circuit court as an adult. During the hearing Carlos did not speak. His court-appointed lawyer entered his guilty plea. He argued self-defense, saying that Carlos had been abused for many years and feared for his life. The numerous scars testified to that and were corroborated by the medical staff at BHMC hospital in North Little Rock, Arkansas. The judge took that into consideration, but the prosecutor had said that Carlos went back to the house seeking revenge. Carlos's lawyer tried to convince the court that Carlos went back for his things and was threatened by his father when he returned. It was convincing; in the end, because of the seriousness of the crime, the jury convicted him of second-degree murder, but the judge suspended sentencing pending a psychiatric evaluation. The evaluation did not reveal much. It didn't seem like the young man wanted to reveal anything further than he had in order to help his situation. Even though Carlos was deemed fit for sentencing, the judge, having seen the extent of the abuse Carlos had suffered, was lenient. He gave him ten years with a chance for parole after seven.

Carlos was the ideal prisoner. He did what he was told and didn't cause any trouble. The only incident was when Carlos was stabbed with a piece of metal that was broken off a piece of industrial laundry equipment. With the metal piece still sticking out of his side, Carlos grabbed the inmate by his neck and picked him up clear off the floor. A group of prisoners stood watching in awe as Carlos slammed him up against the wall and held him there as blood streamed onto the floor. Two guards came rushing over during the commotion, pulled out their clubs, and commanded Carlos to let the man go. Carlos immediately complied, allowing the inmate to drop to the floor like a rag doll. The guards then escorted Carlos to the infirmary, where the physician on shift stitched him back up. Word spread fast in the penitentiary, and after that confrontation, nobody bothered him. Carlos enjoyed five years of quiet contemplation while at the maximum-security facility and then was transferred for good behavior to FCI Forrest City, just eighty-five miles east of Little Rock. It was while serving the remainder of his sentence at FCI that he met Liag, his savior.

CHAPTER 31

"**WAKE UP!**" Gail was shaking Keith vigorously. "What? What!" Keith sat up, eyes glazed over and bloodshot, looking like he had just woken up from a night of partying.

"How can you sleep at a time like this?" she was incensed. "Couldn't you hear the helicopter landing outside?"

"No," Keith murmured. "I am exhausted and hungry. That little bit of beef jerky isn't gonna cut it."

"Shut up and listen," Gail hissed. Keith had never heard Gail speak this way before, and he got quiet more out of shock than from anything she said. "There is a helicopter that just landed maybe fifty to a hundred yards away from us. It may be a rescue attempt. Keith, we need to be ready, and we have to find Taylor. We can't leave without her."

"Well, if it's a rescue, they are being awfully quiet now, since *you* say they came in like Rambo earlier. It's not like the bad guys didn't hear them coming." Keith got up and headed to the bucket. He casually unzipped and began to relieve himself. He seemed so nonchalant about this whole situation. Gail was sickened. *Doesn't he even care that it is his fault we're in this mess? If he hadn't jumped all over the free limo ride and looked into it more carefully, we may have escaped being kidnapped entirely. He did have a point, however,* she thought. *There should be some kind of ruckus if the police had discovered where they were.*

"Keith," she said, looking at him with pleading eyes, "why are you so calm? Aren't you afraid for our lives, for Taylor and what might be happening to her?"

"Of course I'm concerned, honey, but what can we do about it right now? If they wanted to kill us, we would be dead by now. And if we are alive, chances are so is Taylor. I think this is probably one of those kidnappings like in Colombia where a bunch of drug lords kidnap tourists and hold them for ransom. They will probably let us go in a few days. We haven't seen anyone except that hooded guy who brought the food and water, so I don't see why they would need to harm us. It's not like we can finger anyone."

His explanation seemed to make some kind of sense, and it eased Gail's mind at least when it came to Taylor's well-being. But it still didn't seem to make any sense to her from a big-picture perspective. This wasn't South America. This was Hawaii, in the United States of America. These types of things didn't happen for those reasons in America.

She looked over at Keith as he turned away from the bucket zipping up his pants and wondered what she ever saw in him.

CHAPTER 32

AMANDA AND JAKE STOOD LOOKING UP, WAY UP, AT THE LARGE, LOOMING CLIFF WITH A LOT OF SIGNS OF EROSION FORMED FROM ALL THE RAINWATER. "There must be a way around," Jake said to himself.

This can't be, Amanda thought. *How can the path lead directly to the bottom of what looks to be about a three-hundred-foot cliff pretty much straight up?* Both Amanda and Jake were experienced climbers, having ascended many of the rocks around Banff and Canmore in Canada. This wall looked more like the Carstensz Pyramid, one of the Seven Summits and technically more difficult than the rest. This one was not nearly as high, but then again time was of the essence. They had ropes and carabiners, belays, and ascenders and descenders, but they did not have proper climbing shoes, helmets, or body harnesses. Thank goodness there was no snow, because crampons would have been additional weight. They were not expecting to have to climb a cliff this high, nor could they have brought all that equipment with them through the jungle on their mission.

"No wonder they have a helicopter," Jake said, gazing up at the treacherous rocky cliff. "Can you try to *see* another way?" Jake asked in a sarcastic tone.

Amanda at first was ready to lash out but calmed herself. Jake was upset and he had a very sore ankle. The thought of climbing a three-hundred-foot wall of rock was not appealing to her, and she had two good legs. She took a deep breath and let it out slowly before speaking. "Hey, I know this is getting a little crazy, but you can see how wide this cliff is as well as I can. My gift draws me to the victims, but it doesn't give alternate routes. You heard the helicopter. You know that they are up there somewhere. This is nothing compared to Rainier. Now, let's get busy climbing."

"Maybe we should contact Detective Tao. This may be just too far out of our comfort zone now, Amanda. We should get a pretty clear signal on the satellite phone from here, so why not give him a call? He's probably expecting it about now."

Amanda looked up again. "Listen, Jake, if you don't want to go any farther I understand. I can do this. I feel like we are really close, and I can't give up now. If we contact Detective Tao, what will we tell him? That I have a feeling they are on top of a three-hundred-foot cliff? We have nothing concrete. And just for the sake of argument, let's say he does believe us and we give him the GPS coordinates. Do you think he will hike out here or do you think he will bring a team in a helicopter? The bad guys can hear everything we can hear. If they hear a helicopter, they panic and then we will have three dead people on our conscience." Amanda sighed and took a breath. "You can wait for me here or head back. If I am not back with some answers or with Gail, Keith, and Taylor by daybreak, then go for help. I don't want you to take a chance with that ankle of yours."

She was about to continue when Jake put up his hand for her to stop. "I'm all in," was all he said. The look of absolute relief that crossed Amanda's face made Jake smile. She nodded, and they started to set up the gear for the climb. Amanda didn't know what she did to deserve Jake, but she was sure glad they were in this together; somehow it made things just a tiny bit more bearable.

CHAPTER 33

"Voodoo" comes from the word *vodou*, derived from vodŭ, which means spirit or divine creature. It is a syncretic religion, meaning it combines various thoughts and beliefs within its structure and therefore can have many schools of thought when it comes to how best to practice the religion. Carlos remembered studying the differences between Haitian and West African practices, reading about the Supreme Being, called *Bondyè,* and how the deities or *Lwa* (*Loa*) are the true connection to the other world and can help to bring about a good passage to the afterlife. There are many entities that voodooists can worship, and upon meeting Liag and understanding his wisdom, he knew that this was his chance to prove that he was worthy.

Liag was a *bokor*, or priest, which is the highest station in voodoo. He could practice both dark and light, or benevolent, magic as required. "What must be done, must be done," Liag would say. Liag followed the *Petwo* (also *Pethro* and *Petro Loa*) family of spirits. This was a stronger and, according to Liag, more powerful unit that would make the journey to the spiritual realm a certainty.

Carlos thought about the girl who would be sacrificed. Taylor was so young. He remembered asking Liag if there was not another way. But Liag had been adamant, explaining that using virgin blood was the only way, assuring him that while on earth our bodies are nothing but shells, housing the spirit that needs to escape, and that by sacrificing Taylor, both of them would be at peace on the other side. Taylor should feel privileged to be part of the ceremony.

Carlos thought about his spirit and the girl's. "Spirit," Carlos whispered. "Sirpit," he said softly, remembering the name he had used when he rented the car to pick up the family at the airport. He had just moved a letter in the word "spirit" and he had his name.

He thought about the man and woman, greedy and irresponsible. Cleanse the world of these locusts, the Petwo spirits had commanded. They should be happy that they were being put out of their miserable existence. They were small, easy to transport through the jungle, and weak. The drugs had kept them unconscious while they were being transported in the helicopter to the top of the cliff. Carlos had learned a lot from Liag and had been with him longer than any of Liag's other disciples. He would reap the greatest rewards for his loyalty. He felt emotional now that the day had come, the culmination of their efforts. A tear fell from one of the large man's eyes. It ran down his cheek past the long snakes that danced upon his face.

CHAPTER 34

"WHAT ARE YOU DOING?" Jake asked Amanda as she undid the laces on her boots.

"Well, since we don't have any real climbing shoes and, frankly, this is not a hike—it's a straight wall—we are going to have to find all the little fingerholds and toeholds we can in order to get to the top. It's not that high, but it's tricky." She grinned and knew, even though she wasn't looking at Jake, that he was shaking his head.

"OK, monkey girl, whatever turns your crank, but don't come crying to me if you get that fat big toe of yours stuck and we have to cut it off to keep moving."

"Oh, if I'd only cut your foot off in that river," she teased as she undid the second boot and slipped her sock off.

"Well, you had your chance and you blew it." Jake laughed easily, belying the situation they were in. They were about to climb a three-hundred-foot vertical wall with little more than a rope and each other for support. They had to bring the packs with them, which weren't that heavy, but every little bit counts for balance when you are about to go up a wall. Jake and Amanda had tackled quite a few vertical climbs, so technically they were sound. However, those climbs had been in the daytime and with a lot more gear.

Amanda thought about when they tried to summit Mount Rainier, a stratovolcano, which is a mountain built up from many layers, or strata, of hardened lava, located just fifty-four miles southeast of Seattle, Washington. The mountain had three summit points. The lowest one was known as Liberty Cap, at 14,112 feet at the northwestern edge. The second highest was named Point Success, at 14,158, and if you made it to the peak of Columbia Crest, you were at 14,411 feet, the highest summit point. They had all the safety gear and a guide with unsurpassed experience, and yet they found themselves in a serious situation that nearly ended both their lives.

* * *

They had checked into the ranger station at 10:00 a.m. that day in November 2011 and were climbing to Camp Muir, a winter base camp located at ten thousand feet. From there they would summit Columbia Crest. They knew there was supposed to be foul weather, but they weren't expecting whiteout conditions. The wind picked up and the snow was blowing fiercely. Only an hour into it they ran into two other climbers who had just rescued their buddy, who had skied off the ridge. Amanda asked if they needed help, but they said no, and Amanda, Jake, and the guide kept going. Apparently, another couple had radioed for a rescue only a little farther up from Camp Muir as they couldn't see with the whiteout conditions. Amanda and Jake heard the call over their radios and contemplated turning back but decided against it despite the fact that they could barely see each other. They reached Camp Muir in about five and a half hours. There were still some decent winds, but they were finally above the majority of the clouds.

They prepped for dinner, the only expected meal on the mountain besides breakfast the next morning. They woke at 4:00 a.m. to check the weather conditions. Winds were gusty, but the sky was clear—all the clouds were below them and they could see right to Mount Hood and Mount St. Helen; it was spectacular. They began the climb at 6:00 a.m., and by 6:30 a.m. they reached the bottom of Cathedral Gap and switched from skis to mountaineering boots.

At 7:00 a.m. they reached the top of Cathedral Gap, and the guide noticed lenticular clouds in the distance, indicating high winds. They had another discussion on whether they should continue. The guide backed out. He had seen these clouds before and knew that they brought severe weather. He strongly urged Amanda and Jake to turn back and try again the next day. Amanda and Jake had trained hard to do this. They had experienced brutal conditions before and were so close to the top, so they decided to keep going. They put crampons over their boots and moved on. The guide went back to the base camp.

By 8:00 a.m. they were making great time, but the sun had disappeared and clouds were moving in rapidly. By 9:00 a.m. the storm had arrived, but despite roaring winds and whiteout conditions, they were still right on schedule. They were sitting at about twelve thousand feet. However, thirty minutes later the conditions worsened, and although they were attached by rope, they couldn't even see each other. Worse, they couldn't even hear each other over the winds.

By 11:00 a.m. they had slowed down to a crawl. To go up or down at that point made no difference. Each was just as risky, but they would freeze to death if they stopped, so they continued up. The blizzard was incredible; they found out later that gusts had reached ninety-three miles per hour. By 1:30 p.m. they were at 13,850 feet and came across a crevasse. The crevasse was huge, and with zero visibility they couldn't find anywhere to cross.

While they looked futilely for an ice bridge, one of the gusts knocked Jake off his feet. Amanda quickly dropped down to arrest his fall. They had only slid down a few feet. An uncontrolled fall would have meant sliding down thousands of feet or, worse, plummeting into some crevasse, which could have been hundreds of feet of free fall.

Amanda remembered standing up and thinking, *Boy, that was close*, just before she was hit by a ninety-plus-miles-per-hour gust. It blew her right off the ridge. She hurtled down an ice slope, rocketing toward another crevasse just waiting to swallow her about five hundred feet below. Upside down and on her back, Amanda struggled to spin around and flip onto her stomach. Jake had quickly fallen to the ground and dug in his ice ax, but when the rope that tethered them together became taut, he couldn't hold on. Amanda's momentum pulled Jake down the slope too. Picking up speeds reaching thirty miles per hour, they both were wildly trying to dig in their crampons and axes to arrest their fall, breaking the cardinal rule of never arresting a fall with your crampons, as you can break a leg. A broken leg is better than death, so they were trying everything. After about 450 feet, they finally came to a stop, just a few yards from the mouth of the crevasse.

Desperately gripping the axes, with his crampons finally getting into the ice, Jake said, "OK, maybe it's time to turn back." After they caught their breath and their hearts stopped racing, they were able to collect themselves and start their descent back down the mountain with an unsuccessful bid for the summit in their pockets.

At 4:00 p.m. Jake took the lead with visibility still zero. He clambered down a steep ice pitch and began to walk across a flat area when, in mid-step, he disappeared into a fifteen-foot-wide by thirty-five-foot-long crevasse that had been hidden under snow. Amanda dropped down to prepare for the impact of the rope, which was about to become taut, and then a free fall of about forty-five feet. She slid but was able to arrest the fall before following Jake into this seemingly bottomless crevasse.

Amanda built a T-slot with her ice ax in order to use the ax as an anchor and transfer her load, but by the time she was ready, it had filled up with snow and she had to dig again. She couldn't hear anything from Jake and knew she had to keep her mind on the task at hand if Jake was going to survive.

Jake, forty-five feet down, was attempting to quickly ascend the rope and chop away the overhanging lip as he tried to rescue himself. He made his way to an internal snow bridge and was slightly above it when his prusik knot iced up and wouldn't move up or down. He had to cut that cord and fall back down on the rope. He then had to ascend manually or give Amanda rope to Z-pulley him out, which was going to be tough with the overhang. Instead, he decided to climb out until he looked down to see his ice screw missing. It likely came off in the summit fall. So he chose the far side without the overhang and began chopping a ladder with his ice ax.

Meanwhile, Amanda had made a second anchor and built a small snow cave to keep herself warm. Since she hadn't been moving for at least twenty minutes as Jake worked himself out of the crevasse, she was shivering uncontrollably, but at least she was out of the wind. Just when Amanda thought she would lose consciousness, Jake emerged from the crevasse in an impressive free climb that Jake would be able to talk about for years to come.

By 9:30 p.m. they had descended to the final glacier field and were able to ski down to Camp Muir using GPS, since visibility was still poor. They stripped out of their wet gear and huddled together in the sleeping bags they had left in the shelter. It would have been quite romantic if either of them could have stopped shivering long enough to enjoy it.

*   *   *

A shiver ran up Amanda's spine as she remembered that terrifying time on Rainier, and she looked up at the cliff, then over at Jake suddenly, and said, "This is going to be a piece of cake."

CHAPTER 35

"Come, my son," Liag said, waving to Carlos, who was standing obediently at the entrance to the temple. "We have much to prepare for, and the day has started."

Yes, Carlos was fully aware that it was now after midnight, but he was confused. He knew the preparations needed to begin. However, the full moonlight would fall on the seventh, eighth, and ninth days of this new year.

"Carlos, the ritual will happen today, at sunset." The rituals generally began at night and went until dawn. However, Liag had decided they would instead start the ceremony at dawn and end at sunset; he believed the hot spirits would be at their most powerful at that time. "Do not worry," Liag said, as though reading Carlos's mind. "This is the right day; your destiny will not change." Liag was so confident, and Carlos believed him without a doubt. So the day had arrived. Today all his prayers would be answered; today he would feel the glorious freedom he had long waited for, to leave this pestilent mortal world for a world of tranquillity. He would not stop at anything now. It was time, and he was ready.

Liag could see that Carlos was deep in thought. There was no room for reflection; they were running out of time. He knew that there were people coming who had a very good chance of discovering their hideaway. He knew that it wouldn't be long until they arrived to try to rescue the prisoners. All was going according to plan.

The temple was ready. It was a mud-based hut that had taken months to build, with a rounded roof that had a large, circular opening to the sky in the middle. When making a sacrificial offering to the Petwo one was supposed to pay homage properly. There was so much to be done to set up for the ceremony. The altars had to be decorated with white candles and glasses of water for the spirits. Some wildflowers growing nearby had to be picked and placed in various areas around the room in a simple arrangement. Usually it would take a few days to prepare the altar: ritually preparing foods for the service, special cleansings, incantations, lighting candles, and other traditions. However, this was not the type of service they were going to be doing. A voodoo service begins with a series of prayers and songs honoring the saints, followed by a series of verses for all the main spirits of the house. After more introductory songs, beginning with saluting Hounto, the spirit of the drums, the songs for all the individual spirits are sung, starting with the Legba family through all the Rada spirits. Then there is a break, and the Petwo part of the service begins, later ending with the songs for the Gede family.

As the songs are sung, spirits come to visit the ceremony by taking possession of individuals and speaking and acting through them. When a ceremony is held, only the families of those possessed are benefited. In a serious rite, each spirit is saluted and greeted by the initiates present and gives readings, advice, and cures to those who ask for help.

Liag and Carlos had discussed many times where the ritual offerings would be made and that the one who would benefit would be Carlos; his soul would be possessed by the spirits and he would then be taken to the spiritual realm, leaving only his empty carcass behind. However, as Liag had noted several times, the offerings had to be great, and that is why the prisoners were brought there.

"The room is befitting for a most elegant and successful ceremony," Liag said, nodding to Carlos. "You have been devoted, Carlos. This is undisputable. You will be rewarded."

Carlos beamed. He had never been happier in his entire life.

CHAPTER 36

TAYLOR WAS WEAK. She had no idea any longer how much time she had spent in the dungeon, and she could not remember how long ago she had heard the sound of the helicopter, which she now believed was only a hallucination, brought on by starvation and thirst. She had finished her last bit of water about an hour ago, and as with anything else, once it is gone, you seem to need it more. Her throat was dry, and it hurt to swallow.

Her eyes somewhat accustomed to the dark, she looked around the room for something sharp. She wanted to slit her wrists and end the ordeal. She knew that nobody was coming; she had given up hope when she decided the helicopter wasn't real.

As she scanned the room for the umpteenth time, the door slowly creaked open. Her eyes widened and she tried to make herself into a tiny little ball on the floor. She wanted to be sucked right down into the earth, far away from whatever was about to walk through the opening.

It was the hooded figure who had brought her the food earlier. *One of the henchmen*, she thought. A larger version of the Jawa characters in the *Star Wars* movie *A New Hope*. Unfortunately, this giant Jawa was a sign of no hope. *Maybe he has brought some water*, she thought. Her throat was constricted and her mouth watered just from the thought.

Instead, he had a rope in his hands and was coming directly toward her. She gasped and backed right up against the wall. She grabbed at the dirt floor beneath her, trying to hold on to something, but her nails only clawed at loose dirt. The hooded man grabbed her roughly by the arm. She made a weak attempt to struggle but knew it was no use. She had no strength, and her legs gave out even as he pulled her to a standing position. He let her fall back to the ground and tied her hands together. As he made a move to tie her leg, she kicked him in the shoulder, which felt like kicking a solid stone wall, and screamed out, "No! No! No!" With lightning speed he slapped her hard across the face, knocking her to the floor. Shocked into silence, she tasted the blood from her split lip. He picked her up by the legs and held her upside down. The blood rushing to her head made her dizzy. She could feel the drops of blood running down her face toward her eyes; she closed them. He eased her down to the ground and started tying her feet together. Taylor sat up and, with all her might, started hitting him with her tied fists. The hooded figure waited for her to expend all her energy, then he finished tying her feet as she leaned back and broke into small, uncontrollable sobs. The hooded man then easily swung her over his shoulder and headed out the door.

CHAPTER 37

"OH MY GOD!" Gail's heart was beating so hard she felt like it would explode. "That was Taylor. I know it was, Keith."

"Yeah, I heard it too." Keith finally seemed to be registering the depth of the situation they were in. "At least it means she's alive."

"What are you talking about? Are you insane?" Gail seemed on the verge of hysterics. "She was screaming no, Keith. That means something bad was happening to her. Jesus, my baby is in trouble and here we are not able to do anything!" Gail squealed hysterically, making it difficult for Keith to understand her.

"Calm down, Gail. This is no time to lose control. If you don't settle down and think, then we are never going to get out of this situation alive."

"Is that all you can think about right now, how *you* are going to get out of this alive? We're holed up in this prison and those dickheads out there are doing who knows what to my little girl and you stand there and ask me to be calm and think about how we can save ourselves? You're a moron, Keith."

Keith had never heard Gail speak this way before. He had seen her angry, but now she was talking through clenched teeth with spittle flying out as she spoke. Her entire body shook with each word.

"OK, you're right," he said resolutely. "I am a moron, and I feel bad that we can't do anything about this situation or help Taylor right now. But what do you want me to do then, Gail? We have to start thinking about how we can get out. It may be too late to help Taylor, and that's the reality of it."

"If we get out of this alive," she continued through clenched teeth, "I don't ever want to see your face again." With that she turned and put her face in her hands and sobbed helplessly, all the while praying under her breath that Taylor would be OK and for all of them to get out of this alive. Her mind was going through every possible disgusting scenario, and she felt like she was having a nervous breakdown. Keith knew better than to approach her at this point and stood quietly in the corner, wondering how long it would be before their screams would echo through the vast jungle. Just as he was contemplating the possibility of this they heard a key turn in the lock to their dungeon. Gail turned in time to see the door swing open with a loud thud, and through her tears she was able to make out a watery apparition. Standing tall and menacing was the ugliest man she had ever set eyes on, holding a dimly lit lantern. *Are those snakes on his face?* she thought as the beastly creature moved toward them and his large shadow fell across the room.

CHAPTER 38

CLINGING TO A TINY FINGER HOLE WITH HER RIGHT HAND AND SLOWLY FEELING WITH HER LEFT FOR THE NEXT HOLD, AMANDA WAS ABOUT 190 FEET ABOVE THE GROUND. Below her, and attached by about thirty feet of slack rope between them was Jake, waiting for her to take hold and set a cam in place. Amanda wondered how anyone ever did this type of climbing without the use of such gadgets as cams, which are wedged in the rock and spring loaded so that, if a climber fell, it forced the cams to spread and become wedged in place against the rock, securing the climber. They were using the new micro-blasted, spring-loaded camming devices. Amanda would be lead climber until they reached the top, ensuring that each point was secured. Jake would belay, taking up rope or giving Amanda rope as needed and picking up the protection placed along the way up.

It was dark, but the moon was amazingly bright, even though it would not be a full moon for a few more nights. For now it offered plenty of light to make their climb less treacherous, but it was unnerving all the same. Amanda gazed at the sky for a moment, thinking that this could have been one of the most serene and beautiful nights they had ever spent together, if it weren't for the fact that they were under extreme time constraints trying to save their friends' lives. "Hey, stargazer, move your ass," Jake buzzed in through the ear piece. They both had their voice-activated Motorola radios. Needing their hands to climb, they could not rely on push-to-talk technology, so it was a good thing they upgraded the units prior to the trip. Amanda thought it must be at least one o'clock in the morning. She hadn't checked her watch for some time, and doing so at that moment probably was not a good idea, so she continued up, scaling the wall with better-than-average skill, her bare feet clinging with the ease of a native climbing a tree.

They were simpatico, climbing together as one, so they made good progress, and this gave Amanda hope that they would get to their friends in time.

As she was considering her next hold, it suddenly seemed as if someone had turned off the lights. Darkness and quiet surrounded them, and then a slight breeze started up. "Oh shit!" Jake's voice was in her ear. Amanda turned slightly to see that the moon had been enshrouded by a large, black, cumulus nimbus, otherwise known to both of them as a BBC—big black cloud.

"Of all the luck. I knew it was just too good to be true," Amanda muttered as the wind picked up. It was a climber's worst nightmare: complete darkness, high winds, and, just when they thought it couldn't get any worse, rain—light at first and then in harsh, hammering sheets.

Jake noticed that there was a crack in the wall face a few feet over that was large enough to wedge themselves into. This gave them the ability to climb faster in a synchronized crouch by using their backs and legs against the inside walls of the crack. The rain, however, was coming down in full force and turned the crack into a funnel. Water rushed down over the tops of them. Amanda felt like she couldn't breathe, like she was sitting under a waterfall and couldn't move just from the sheer pressure of the water.

Jake yelled as loud as he could, but it still sounded like he was miles away from the radio. "We have to find somewhere to stop for a bit until this lets up." Amanda nodded and realized Jake couldn't see her. She was having trouble keeping her eyes open. The rain stung as it relentlessly beat down on them, and they clung to the side of the now slippery wall face.

"Looks like there is a small ledge up about thirty feet," Amanda radioed back down, hoping the rain wouldn't drown out her words. The ledge was a piece of rock jutting out about two feet from the wall face. They started ascending toward the ledge when, suddenly, the entire rock lit up like a movie screen. *Oh, Jesus*, Amanda thought. *Lightning*.

*   *   *

The worst thing you can encounter while hanging on the face of a flat rock is lightning. Jake and Amanda were very aware of this from the many times they had climbed and the training they had received. The best thing for them to do would be to head back down, but that would certainly be to the detriment of the family who was hoping to be rescued. They were nearly two-thirds of the way to the top, and Amanda's senses were that if they turned back now, they would be taking just as much of a chance as if they continued, and they would have to give up their mission to save their friends as well.

The ledge would leave them completely exposed at a dangerous height, perfect targets for a lightning strike, but they also knew it was imperative to get all the gear off. The wet ropes were a fabulous way of carrying current, and wrapped around the two of them, it would be a sure way to get zapped.

It was now a matter of life and death to get to the ledge. They moved quickly, and neither one of them spoke or stopped to take a breather. Amanda was getting down to the last few pieces of gear on her rack, but she was sure Jake was cleaning the route, collecting all her gear as they went up, so they would have no problem topping out if they could get through this thunderstorm.

It was time for Jake to take the lead. Amanda secured herself to the station and radioed down: "Secure." She waited for Jake, the seconder, to take her off belay. Jake started up. He reached the ledge and then climbed up beyond it to set up a secure station above the ledge. This would secure them in case they slipped off the ledge. He then side-climbed over to the ledge and dropped down. He took off the gear pack, which had been converted easily into a backpack for the climb, and rested it at the back of the ledge, which was barely wide enough to hold the pack. He waited for Amanda to ascend, but just as she came past the ledge, they heard a loud crash, then a bang, and a tree that was on the top of the cliff above them exploded. A branch came hurtling down, right at Amanda.

CHAPTER 39

THE LARGE SHADOW MOVED QUICKLY TOWARD KEITH, AND WITH ONE QUICK BLOW THE GIANT STRUCK KEITH HARD ON THE HEAD WITH THE HILT OF A VERY LARGE KNIFE. In fact, it looked like a sword of some sort. Gail screamed such a high-pitched scream that at first she didn't realize it was coming from her. Then she started sobbing as she realized there was nothing she could do to stop what was happening to them.

Another hooded figure, obviously the leader, stepped into the room behind the man with the snake tattoos and stayed in the shadow and pointed as a third hooded shape slid past them and, exhibiting incredible strength, quickly swung Keith's unconscious body over his shoulder and walked out.

"What do you want?" she stammered, knowing that she wasn't going to get an answer but also instinctively trying to postpone the inevitable. "We don't have money with us, but we can get you some." The man in the shadows walked up behind the large man and whispered something, then turned and left the room. The large man nodded at Gail and pointed the long sword to the door. Gail realized that this meant for her to leave the room and follow the other man. She walked quickly, but her legs felt like Jell-O. She wasn't sure if she would be able to walk, but the sharp point of the sword on her back gave her strength.

CHAPTER 40

HER HEAD HURT, AND HER EYESIGHT WAS BLURRY, BUT TAYLOR COULD TELL THEY HAD MOVED HER ABOUT A HUNDRED YARDS OUT- SIDE. It was still dark, and in the distance she heard thunder. The breeze picked up, and a few large drops of rain hit her back as she was jostled up and down to the rhythm of the man carrying her.

She thought she could hear her mom sobbing, but that must have been her imagination, or was it? After all, her mom and Keith had to be somewhere around here. She tried to lift her head to scan the area, but her head felt like a bowling ball, heavy and hard to lift. She seemed to have no strength, and looking down at the ground started to make her dizzy. She felt like she was going to throw up, and frankly she hoped she would, all over the thug who was carrying her. As her thoughts were engaged in how sick she was feeling, they entered another building of sorts. Like her prison cell, it had dirt walls and was dank-smelling, but this one had a long, torch-lit cor- ridor that led to a large, round room with a circular hole in the center where the roof should have been. The hooded thug roughly dropped her to the ground and then turned and left. Taylor looked up to see torches burning all around the perimeter of the room, and candles formed shadows all over the walls and floor. The bright light hurt her eyes after she had been in the dark for so long. Rain soaked a large, flat slab of stone that sat on a pedestal under the hole.

Around the large stone slab were smaller stone tables with candles and white flowers arranged around them. There were also glasses of water on a few of the tables, which Taylor would have found strange except that she was so thirsty and thought it was a mirage of some sort. She tried to drag herself along the floor to get closer to one of the tables with the water. A large shadow crossed her. She looked up at the wall and saw a large man. She slowly rolled onto her back and looked toward the entrance to the room. Filling the doorway was the man with the snakes tattooed on his face. He was holding a large sword. The light from the torches glinted off its blade as he moved toward her.

CHAPTER 41

DETECTIVE TAO TOSSED AND TURNED. It was four in the morning, and he decided sleep was futile. He kept thinking about the Bannons and the fact that he had heard nothing from them. He was now certain he was going to be looking for five missing people.

He got up and put on a pot of coffee before taking a quick shower. Then he got dressed, poured himself some coffee, and sat down at his desk. He opened the file marked "Wright/Stevens" and started going over the various reports.

What am I missing? he thought. It was a pretty cut-and-dry case so far. A family holiday gone wrong. The crime rate was very low on the islands for violent crimes, and especially for this sort of thing. Kidnappings didn't usually happen in Hawaii, and when they did they were almost always domestic cases—divorced parents taking a child because they didn't get custody rights or an ex-boyfriend who didn't want to lose his girlfriend. Those didn't typically turn out so good. He had worked through all the details of the investigation so far and hoped he would get a break soon. So far every leaf he turned over revealed very little that would help in this case. He had received a call earlier in the day from the chief, who wasn't pleased with the lack of results. Tao had his entire team working on everything from background checks to witnesses, trying to fit all the pieces together, and it was taking way too long.

Bernie Wright had seemed very upset when they spoke the previous morning. Detective Tao thought about his statement that the local authorities weren't doing enough to find out what had happened to his ex-wife and child. Wright had already gone up the food chain, and Detective Tao was getting plenty of pressure from the top dogs.

He thought about the Bannons and wondered what they had found and why they hadn't contacted him yet. He started to believe that they were his only hope of getting close to finding these people and solving this mystery. He felt a bit embarrassed about how he had treated Amanda Bannon. Now all he could do was wait until morning and set out after them. He had an idea of where they were and decided it was time to start getting his shit together and go after them. He would have to make some phone calls and arrange a helicopter and some backup. He was pretty sure the FBI would want to get involved, since they were dealing with Canadians kidnapped in the U.S., and the RCMP would be pressuring the U.S. government for answers. It would take a few hours to get a helicopter and search party together, more than a few hours—the system was slow, even in an emergency situation. How long had it been since the family had disappeared? It was going on the fourth day. *Hmmm*, he thought, *generally if we don't find them within the first forty-eight hours, we're looking for corpses.* However, he knew that it depended on the purpose of the kidnapping, if there *was* a purpose. There were cases of insane stalkers, delusional people who committed crimes for no apparent reason. Sometimes people on the edge were allowed to run free because there was no social infrastructure in place to actually get them into treatment for their psychological issues, so money continued to be wasted as the authorities dealt with the consequences of not resolving the core issues. He ran his hand through his thick, mostly gray hair, collected the files, and headed toward the door. *Might as well do this at the office*, he thought.

CHAPTER 42

LIAG WATCHED IN THE SHADOWS AS THE STEVENS MAN WAS CAR-
RIED TO A ROOM NEXT TO THE CEREMONIAL CHAMBER. He would be
regaining consciousness soon, and that was good. Liag wanted him to be
awake when they began the events of this very special day. Carlos, who only
knew what Liag had taught him, was on the verge of completing the last
stage of his mission to move into the afterworld. As he supervised Carlos's
final preparations, Liag thought back to the beginning of his relationship
with Carlos at FCI Forrest City minimum-security prison.

During their first meeting, Liag could tell right away that Carlos was a
man who harbored resentment against everybody and everything. He knew
all about Carlos's past—what he had done to his father and why. He knew
everything about this young man who needed an outlet, something that
would give him what he was missing all his life: a father and a purpose.

Liag strategically spent time with Carlos. He knew that Carlos needed
something to believe in. Liag had spent many months studying and reading about the various religious families of voodoo and knew that this might
be his way of getting Carlos hooked into helping him with his mission. At
first there was nothing: no response, no communication. As Liag started to
talk about another world, one that would take away all the hurt and pain,
and introduced some of the practices of the religion, Carlos began paying
attention.

Eventually, Carlos started asking questions. He wanted to know how he could join the religion and who he should pray to in order to leave this world and enter the spiritual one. That was when Liag knew he would be able to train Carlos in all that he had been studying. He spent more than a year visiting Carlos on a regular basis, teaching and showing him the rituals and rites of the Petwo. Liag was tender and patient with Carlos and gained his undying trust. That, he knew, was the key to ensuring that in the end all his plans would come to fruition.

The toughest part of Liag's plan was Carlos's escape from the prison. He would only be able to do so much to assist Carlos, and the rest would be up to the big man himself. It all came together one night. Liag made sure that Carlos was assigned to laundry duty. Liag had friends on the inside; bribery was easy if you knew the right people to talk to. Liag had the confidence of another inmate who worked laundry detail. Liag offered to get some money to his family if he would help Carlos. Once Carlos was safely inside a laundry cart, the other inmate threw a few bed sheets and towels on top of him and transferred him to the laundry truck, which carried him out of the prison gates. The guard watching the area was distracted by a fight going on between the bribed inmate and two others. The truck was five miles away before the guard realized he was short one man.

The next day they found the laundry truck abandoned on a back road near Little Rock. The driver was tied up and gagged with ripped bed sheets. He was dehydrated and hungry but otherwise fine. They knew how the prisoner had escaped, but how far he had gotten nobody knew. It was much farther than anyone could have imagined.

Liag had given Carlos a map to the safe house where they met, and Liag was waiting with a change of clothes. First, he dyed Carlos's hair a sandy brown and gave him blue contact lenses. He had doctored a photo ahead of time and had a fake ID and passport already made up with Carlos's new look. They drove forty hours straight through from Arkansas to Washington State, each sleeping while the other one drove. Liag set up Carlos in a small apartment with plenty of reading material on the religion of voodoo. Carlos took his new beliefs very seriously.

A few days later Liag came to set up the Internet in the apartment and was shocked to see Carlos had shaved his head and tattooed his face with snakes, of all things. When Liag asked why he had chosen to change his appearance so drastically, Carlos explained that he wanted to be clean shaven all over when he entered the new world, but he also wanted never to forget the pain and the poison that was his life on earth. The snakes symbolized the dark world he would leave behind. Liag understood, and, besides, his new menacing look would be perfect for the job at hand.

Liag spent some time showing Carlos how to find information on the Internet and how Google worked. Carlos was fascinated; he had never had the opportunity as a child to learn about computers. Now he spent hours in front of his new toy, and soon Liag gave him his first task toward their mission. It started with an e-mail address: tayloranneewright@hotmail.com.

CHAPTER 43

AS SOON AS AMANDA HEARD THE CRASH, SHE LOOKED UP TO SEE A LARGE BRANCH BOUNCE OFF THE ROCK FACE TEN FEET ABOVE HER. She managed to move just in time, but part of the branch glanced off her left arm, and although it ripped her sleeve at the lower arm, the cut went from her wrist to about midway up her forearm. She had yet to feel the pain from the cut as adrenalin pumped through her. When Jake saw the branch come tumbling down, he instinctively tried to grab Amanda and pull her in toward him. In his haste, he nudged his pack with his right leg and watched helplessly as it fell the two hundred fifty-something feet, crashing at the bottom, he assumed with tremendous force.

"Jesus H. Christ!" he screamed, more upset with himself than at the situation. He knew to consider all aspects of a situation, but his judgment always seemed to get clouded when Amanda's safety was involved. He should have just trusted her to get out of the way, just like she did; now he was going to have to let her know that half their survival gear was crushed at the bottom of the wall.

Amanda had blood running down her arm. As the rain washed most of it away, she could see that the gash was deeper than she first imagined. Her first thought, however, was to get on the ledge with Jake and then take a careful look at it. She was making her way over when thunder roared and then another bolt of lightning lit up the wall face. A few seconds later thunder cracked. The good news was that the lightning was farther away now. Those types of crazy thunderstorms generally came and went quickly in the South Pacific.

Jake gently helped Amanda onto the ledge, and she quickly removed all her gear and ropes. They put everything on the far side of the ledge, including Amanda's backpack. She looked around quizzically, so Jake piped up right away: "It's gone."

"Great, how did that happen?" she asked, not really wanting an answer but knowing he would want to explain regardless.

"Well, I was reaching out to pull you in when that branch fell down, and I accidently kicked it off the ledge."

Amanda was upset. Jake carried the satellite phone in his pack, along with some of the heavier items, like ammo and ropes. Generally, they wouldn't need most of the stuff in the pack, but it's always the one time you don't have something that you need it.

"Shit happens," was all Amanda managed to get out.

"OK, let's take a look at that arm." Jake moved next to Amanda and pulled back the ripped sleeve. "Nice one. What do you have for first aid?" Amanda always carried the lighter stuff: first aid, water purification pills, EpiPens, and medications. Jake pulled Amanda's pack over and took out some rubbing alcohol and poured it on the wound. Amanda closed her eyes and tightened her grip on the piece of rock she was leaning against, but she didn't make a sound. Jake pulled out some gauze and surgical tape and cut a piece large enough to hold Amanda's wound together. "It could use stitches, but this will do if you try to stay out of trouble."

"Nah, no stitches required. It's just a flesh wound," Amanda retorted. She smiled, but she was feeling far from happy with the situation. They were in the worst place on the planet to be in the middle of a lightning storm, on a ledge in a rock face. They were exhausted, but they couldn't lie down because if lightning did strike it would travel through the rock and, if they were lying down, it would run right through their bodies—not good. The best position for them was to crouch or squat down on either side of the ledge, away from the gear and ropes, then pray that the storm would subside quickly so they could get on their way.

Jake looked over at Amanda crouched down on the ledge, with her bare feet and taped arm. He thought she looked so small, but he knew she was tough enough to get through this. Then he silently reprimanded himself again for dropping the pack. He hoped they would have enough ammunition. He had been smart enough to move the gun back to the inside pocket of his jacket, where he had a strap to hold it. He had decided it was best to have it concealed but close at hand. Never know what you're gonna run into out in the middle of the jungle.

CHAPTER 44

TAYLOR WAS SO AFRAID OF THE LOOMING GIANT WITH THE SWORD
WHO CAME TOWARD HER THAT SHE HADN'T EVEN SEEN THE SMALLER
FIGURE HUDDLED IN FRONT OF HIM MOVING INTO THE ROOM. Then
she heard, "Oh my God, Taylor? Are you OK, honey?"

Carlos allowed the woman to rush over to the girl and console her. He
figured it wouldn't make any difference, that the ceremonial sacrifice would
be under way soon and this would all be over.

"Mom, oh, Mom." Taylor's sobs were so dire and needy that Gail broke
down and cried too. "I'm so sorry, Mom," she managed. "This is all my fault."

"How can any of this be your fault, sweetie?" Gail was now brushing
her fingers through Taylor's fine blonde hair to soothe her, just like she used
to when Taylor was upset when she was younger.

"I led this creep to us," Taylor stammered. "I met him on the Internet. I
told him we were coming to Hawaii and when. That's how he found us. He
had the car waiting for us, but I don't know who all these other people are in
the long robes and hoods."

Gail was surprised to hear all this but knew no reprimand was going to
get them out of the current situation, and her daughter was already in hysterics. She couldn't believe they were in this situation because of an Internet
relationship. She had given Taylor the talk over the years. Bernie used to tell
them about weirdos they arrested who were seducing young people over the

Internet. They had set up sting operations in which cops would begin a chat with these creeps, saying they were twelve or thirteen. When the perverts would take the conversation to a sexual level, the cops would lure them to a sting house. The cops would claim their parents were out for the afternoon and invite the creep over for sex. That was all it would take to put them away for some time.

Gail thought the snake man didn't fit the usual pedophile-sicko profile, although something about him was way out in left field. Why go through all the trouble of kidnapping an entire family and then taking them out to the middle of nowhere? And what was with all the costumes? Gail looked around the torch-lit room, scoping everything out. *This looks like some kind of ritual scene out of the movies, with the stone altars and candles lit everywhere*, she thought. "Oh my God," she whispered.

"What? What is it?" Taylor asked in a terrified voice. "Mom, what's wrong?"

"N–n–nothing," Gail stammered as she continued to smooth down Taylor's hair, but in her mind she saw all those old movies with the blonde virgin tied to the flat stone altar as the evil witch doctors and painted hedonistic pagans chanted and danced around waiting for the right time to sacrifice the child.

CHAPTER 45

THE THUNDER AND LIGHTNING STRIKES WERE GROWING FARTHER APART, AND THE RAIN LET UP. In the distance there was a soft glow on the horizon. Dawn was coming. "What time is it?" Amanda asked.

Jake checked his watch. "Quarter after five. It is gonna start getting light in about an hour and a half. How's the arm?"

Amanda looked down at her taped-up forearm. "Good. It stopped bleeding, and I think I can feel most of my fingers."

"Well, you only need a couple to climb with, and you have your other hand and your monkey feet. That's like having another set of arms for you, isn't it?"

"Whatever. Stop exercising your lips and let's finish this wall. My legs and butt are killing me from that crouch. It's gonna feel good to stretch back out on the rock."

Jake nodded. "I'm sure glad we spent all that time doing those wall squats during our workouts. Never thought it would come in handy, but who knew?" He took the lead, and they finished the climb at a good speed, climbing the final thirty or so feet in under an hour.

At the top Amanda pulled out another Clif Bar and split it in half, throwing one half to Jake, who caught it in one hand with ease while continuing to get out of his climbing gear with the other. They put as much of their gear as they could into Amanda's pack but had to leave some of the heavier pieces of climbing gear and rope behind. They couldn't manage to take everything without the second pack. Amanda removed her boots, which had been tied to the outside of her pack. They were soaked. She pulled out her socks, which were stuffed into the boots, and wrung them out. Even though her socks and boots were wet, it beat walking through the jungle barefoot, so she slid her feet into the boots.

"Hopefully we're not gonna need this stuff again, unless we have to come back this way. I doubt anyone is going to come along and take it, but just to be sure . . ." Jake moved the climbing gear and rope toward some brush and then threw some nearby branches and palm leaves on top.

"Yeah, 'cause nobody could tell you're hiding something under that big pile of leaves and stuff," Amanda said with a snicker.

Jake gave her a look and walked away from the pile. "OK, psychic, which way to the party?"

Amanda looked around, then nodded to her right. "Jake, I don't think it's going to be far. We should get prepared." Jake knew exactly what Amanda meant and removed his Glock from his inner pocket. He now wore the one pack they had left between the two of them on his back. Amanda reached into it and took out her smaller snub nose. They both knew that it was time to get down to business, and without the satellite phone they didn't have any connection to the outside world. Any assistance would have to come by way of a miracle. They did a radio check so that the two of them could at least stay in communication, because it was likely that they would have to split up if they were to have any chance at all of saving their friends.

CHAPTER 46

KEITH'S VISION WAS BLURRY, AND HE CAME TO WITH A LARGE GOOSE EGG ON THE FRONT OF HIS FOREHEAD WHERE THE LARGE MAN HAD HIT HIM WITH THE HEAVY HILT OF THE SWORD. As his vision came into focus, he saw a figure sitting just ten or so feet in front of him on a chair. Keith tried to get up from the floor but fell back down as a bout of vertigo swept over him, no doubt from the blow to his head. He felt nauseous, and his mouth was as dry as the Sahara Desert.

"What the fuck is going on?" he managed to blurt out to the hooded figure across from him. He was trying to sound tough but not even coming close. "What is this all about? Do you know who I am?"

"We know who you are." The hooded figure spoke in a hushed voice, as though he were trying to be quiet but needed to be heard.

"Well, you know I'm an officer with the RCMP then, and what you are doing is going to get you in more shit than you can imagine. You're not dealing with just a regular civilian. They will come down on you hard, you know. The FBI is probably tearing this area apart looking for me."

"That is to be seen." The voice was even deeper and slower. Keith strained forward to hear.

"Who are you? Tell me what you want. You can still get out of this. I have connections that will make this a whole lot easier on you if you let me go now." Keith was speaking rapidly now. He felt like he was running out of time to get his points across. He wasn't sure, but he had a helpless feeling, like something heavy was about to fall on him and crush him and he couldn't do anything about it. His stomach ached like he needed to be sick, but he was too scared to move.

"What about the women?" The hushed voice sounded curious.

"Are they still alive?" Keith looked around, like he would see Taylor and Gail watching him from somewhere in the room. "Do you want them for something? Listen, I don't know what the hell is going on here. You kidnapped us for a reason, and if it's the women you want, well, frankly you have the upper hand here. I mean, what am I supposed to do, fight you and that giant snake-faced guy you have working for you? It's obvious that you have plans, and if they don't include me, then we can work something out, right?"

"No need." The voice was dark and ominous.

"What do you mean, no need? You don't need me? Or you're gonna let me go, so there is no need for me to do anything for you? I don't get it." He tried to lift himself off the ground, when the figure suddenly stood up and moved closer to him.

"You will die." The figure was now standing only a few feet away from Keith, and he knew without a doubt that this man was not lying. Keith felt sweat break out all over his body as the dark-hooded man walked slowly toward him. He tried to scramble backward as the hooded man pulled out a handgun from beneath his robe. The man was now close enough for Keith to see the gun. His eyes went wide with terror and then confusion: a 9mm Smith & Wesson 5946 pistol, something that Keith was extremely familiar with.

"Wh-wh-where did you get that gun?" Keith was blubbering now. His face was contorted as the man pointed the gun at him, then he reached up toward the hooded figure with both arms outstretched in a pleading manner. "No . . . no, it can't be. This can't be happening!" His head was swirling with thoughts, and then he knew, he understood, he grew calm.

He looked up as the man with the gun pulled the hood back from his face, and there was absolutely no surprise in the look Keith had on his face when the bullet entered his forehead, leaving a large hole about the size of a baseball in the back of his head.

CHAPTER 47

GAIL WAS STILL CONTEMPLATING THE USES OF THE STONE ALTAR AND THE SHARP SWORD THE SNAKE-FACED MAN WAS CARRYING WHEN HE WALKED OVER AND HAULED HER UP OFF THE FLOOR.

"It's time," he said in such a calm manner it terrified Gail.

"Time for what?" she said, spitting out the words. "You have had us holed up here for days. We have had little food and water, and now what can you possibly expect from us at this point?" She knew it was useless asking these questions, but she felt she had to show some kind of strength, for Taylor's sake. She wanted her little girl to feel protected in some way, even though she knew the chances of them escaping were close to zero.

"Time for you to prepare the girl for the ceremony, the sacrifice, the end that will create the beginning." Carlos turned and pointed to the stone altar, then to the roof where the early rays of dawn were just starting to show through the round opening.

Taylor started to shake. Gail quickly circled her arms around her and tried to think. What could she do? She could try to jump this huge man, but then she would be dead in seconds and Taylor would be left on her own, and Gail couldn't do that to her. Gail was wishing she had some kind of poison pill or something that she and Taylor could take so these pigs wouldn't have the luxury of taking their lives. She was imagining how difficult it would be to commit suicide when they heard a loud gunshot.

Carlos turned quickly toward the sound. He knew that Liag was with the man named Keith, who must have gotten out of hand. Liag was peaceful and would use violence only when necessary to get the attention of the spirits that were going to help take their dream to realization. They had spoken many times about how they would use violence as a last resort, but as a much-needed avenue if anyone got in the way of their plans. The sacrifice of the young girl was not violence; it was a beginning for all of them. Carlos was a little confused. When he and Taylor had corresponded via e-mail, he had often gone over the rites and rituals of the religion. He thought she fully understood what was needed, yet now she was upset and not cooperating in the manner in which he had hoped she would. Never mind. She had no choice but to fulfill her obligation at this point.

Gail didn't want to think about the gunshot. She knew Keith was close by in another mud building, and the sound seemed to come from that direction. "Oh, God, help us," she groaned into Taylor's hair.

"God cannot help you," the man said calmly, "and God did not help him." He nodded in the direction of where Keith had been.

Gail burst into tears. She couldn't hold back anymore. She kept replaying in her mind like a marquee at a movie theater the last words she had vehemently uttered to Keith before they were taken out of the dungeon: "I don't ever want to see your face again."

CHAPTER 48

DETECTIVE TAO WENT OVER THE FILES AGAIN, THEN HE WENT BACK OVER THE CONVERSATIONS HE'D HAD WITH AMANDA BANNON. He remembered her saying that Taylor Wright was having an Internet relationship with a man named Carlos. The man who rented the car that picked up the family at the airport was named Carlos. They were involved in some kind of voodoo-religion chat together for months, and now she and her family were missing.

The RCMP officer who first notified the department was Bernie Wright, the ex-husband of Gail Wright and the father of Taylor Wright. Gail and Bernie had been divorced for more than two years, and the girl and this Carlos person had been in touch for at least six months.

Detective Tao had something that kept niggling at him. He couldn't put his finger on it, but he decided to take a flier and make some phone calls. He still had some pretty good connections with some of the boys in the Honolulu office.

"Hey, Tony, it's me, Ron Tao."

"Hey, Ron! How are you, man? It's early, buddy. I'm just getting out of bed. You guys getting lonely out there on the Big Isle? You gotta call us homies for some company, or what?" the friendly voice on the other end said with a chuckle.

"No, man," Detective Tao said in a no-nonsense tone; he could visualize

Anthony Ramos on the other end straightening up to listen. "I got a problem. You probably heard we're looking for a missing family out here."

"Yeah, yeah. We know about that one. Tough. Young girl involved, huh? I heard you got some kind of psychic helping you out too. Don't know about that stuff, man; I say stick to the facts."

"Hey, no shit, I am trying my best to stick to the facts, but we don't have too much to go on. This Bannon lady apparently has helped solve a few cases before. If nothing else, it can't hurt . . . Well, if they stay alive, it can't hurt." Tao sighed.

Tony could hear the frustration in his friend's voice, and he understood what it was like to feel helpless in this type of situation, so he eased up. "Hey, man, what can I do for you? Just let me know."

"I was hoping we could get some intel—you know, some background—on some of the players involved. I know lots on this Bannon couple. They come highly recommended, and they are clean as a whistle. I am trying to find out more about this Keith Stevens and Bernie Wright, both RCMP officers."

"No problem, man. I am good friends with a guy in Edmonton. I met him while he was on vacation here many years ago. We became close. I used to go watch the Edmonton Oilers kick ass in hockey back in the days of Gretzky and Messier." Tony was about to go on with his story of the glory days when Tao cut in. "Hey, love to hear all about it over a cold one soon, but we're running out of time on this one." He let his words trail off, giving them the effect he knew they would have on Tony.

"I'm on it, buddy. Give me a few hours and I should be able to get some information at least on the history of these guys."

"Great, thanks, Tony. I really appreciate the help, and, oh, one last thing: see if there is any connection with either of these guys to the name Carlos, anything at all, no matter how small, OK?"

"You got it, amigo. Sit tight." With that, Tony hung up. Tao sat there for a moment. "Sit tight, huh? Yeah, right."

He picked up the phone and dialed his assistant. "Stephanie, get the paperwork done. I'm gonna need a helicopter and pilot pronto." He sat back and watched the dawn of another day, which meant even less of a chance of saving those people from whatever fate was awaiting them.

CHAPTER 49

A LARGE FLOCK OF BIRDS FLUTTERED STRAIGHT UP IN FRONT OF
AMANDA AND JAKE IN A PANIC AT THE SOUND OF A GUN BLAST THAT
RICOCHETED OFF THE WALLS OF THE HILLS ON ALL SIDES. Amanda
was startled for a second, then looked over at Jake, who had a pained expres-
sion on his face, which said it all. They might be too late.

She waved him forward, and he crouched as they moved in unison
toward the sound. She figured it was about a half mile off. Amanda's heart
was beating so hard she could hear it in her ears. It almost sounded like
footsteps right behind her, and she had to suppress the urge to keep looking
back. *Nothing there but the cliff,* she reminded herself.

Jake pointed at something just to his left up high. Amanda moved in
slowly to see a large wooden mask nailed to the trunk of a tree, probably
symbolizing the entry point of a territory. Amanda had studied cultural reli-
gions in college, and from what she could remember, it was a mask of the
Egungun people and was part of a West African ceremony to bring together
the elusive spiritual world with the world of the living, normally through
dance and drums.

Jake whispered into his radio, "Know anything about that?" His eyes
were glancing back up at the mask.

Amanda nodded, then whispered back into her mouth bud, "Yup, voodoo mask that speaks to the cult of the dead."

Jake's eyes widened, but he said nothing more. At least he didn't roll his eyes. She knew what he thought of cults, religion, and anything else where people abused power by manipulating others for their own gain. He had seen this to the most infinite degree with Roman Catholics. She couldn't blame him, and although she felt connected to another world somehow with her gift, she knew there had to be a logical explanation and tried to understand it with reason and common sense. They were both realists, like Thomas Paine, and often quoted lines from *The Age of Reason* when it came to discussions with friends about religion. Most times they would opt out completely of religious debates because they would rather be dealing in facts.

They continued to move closer to the compound and found a spot under some bushes to lie down and survey the scene. Daylight was slowly making it nearly impossible for them to stay hidden within the dark brush, but things were quickly coming to a head regardless. Amanda pulled out a small set of binoculars and could now just make out the shapes among the hills and brush. It looked to be a small group of buildings made of mud. In West Africa, mud buildings were very common and had been around for thousands of years. If kept up, they were very sustainable structures and provided protection from both heat and cold. One of the buildings was larger than the rest, and Amanda thought it looked like an oval pot, like you would make in pottery class. It was farther up the hill than the rest of the buildings. Through the binoculars she peered to the left of the oval building and could just make out the Bell 206. *Yep, Jake hit the nail on the head as usual,* Amanda thought. When it came to aircraft, he knew his stuff. She could see a lone dark figure walking toward the large oval building. It looked like someone wearing a monk's outfit. She handed the binoculars to Jake, who quickly scanned the scene. "Looks like they have a couple of security checkpoints," he whispered. He then pointed left and right of them. Amanda was startled to see a robed figure about fifty yards away on either side of them and another one slightly ahead of them in the clearing. They were all carrying what looked to be M16 military assault rifles.

"Split up?" Jake whispered. Amanda nodded and took her gun with the full clip, wishing she had some of the extra clips that were lost during their climb. She took the binoculars from Jake and slipped them into her pocket with the knife she had used earlier in the river.

"Meet up twenty-five yards in the brush behind the oval building," she said, so quietly Jake had to mostly read her lips. He nodded, and they headed out in opposite directions, hoping they wouldn't run into any more sentries around the perimeter on the way to the meeting place on the other side.

As they started out, Amanda got a head rush that made her dizzy. She thought she was going to fall, but she stopped only for a second as she knew Jake would be making good time. They would keep radio silence unless an emergency happened, and Amanda did not consider the dizzy spell an emergency, but she knew it was an indication that she was going to have another vision or premonition. She was considering the best route around a large fallen tree that would give her cover and, at the same time, trying to fend off the dizziness. She closed her eyes and gasped at the vision in her head of the blood-splattered walls of a mud hut and a river of blood running down the face of Keith Stevens.

CHAPTER 50

DAYLIGHT MADE ITS WAY INTO THE ROUND ROOM AS GAIL AND TAYLOR HUDDLED ON THE FLOOR. Carlos could see that the woman was trying to slowly untie the ropes that bound the girl's hands and feet, but he wasn't concerned. *Soon enough their fate will be sealed*, he thought. He could hear footsteps approaching behind him and turned to see Liag enter the round room.

Liag came over and whispered into his ear; he nodded and walked over to Gail and Taylor. "Come," he said. The sword was held at his side but not in any threatening manner. Gail and Taylor stood up. Taylor now was bound only by the ropes at her hands. Gail had untied her feet while Liag was whispering to Carlos.

Taylor was weak. Her mother had to support her while she walked. Carlos pointed to a hallway on the other side of the room. The hallway led to a door. Gail pushed the door open to reveal a tiny area barely big enough for the three of them to stand in. The only light came from a very small round hole, much like the ones in the other rooms where they had been held. There was enough light to see a bowl of water, what looked like a small towel, and a long, plain white dress. In the early morning light they were able to make out that the walls were made of some kind of mud or clay. *What the hell is this place?* Gail thought, as Carlos followed them in.

Carlos had to duck to get into the room. He pointed to the area where the water and dress lay. "Clean the child and dress her. She must be ready when the time comes."

"Why? What's the difference? Can't you put her on the altar the way you found her?" Gail knew she was being irrational now, but anything to delay the steps in this process was a victory to her at this point.

"If you do not have her washed and dressed in an hour when I return, I will have to do it myself. If that is how you want to proceed, that is fine. We have no time to waste. The ceremony will start shortly, and the spirits will not be as generous as we have been. If you are not ready, we will be forced to offer them something more quickly to appease them, and that will be you."

He pointed the sword at Gail, and Taylor immediately burst into tears again. Gail knew it would be better to just obey. At least it would buy them another hour.

"OK, OK, can you give us some privacy, and can I take the ropes off her hands?"

"Yes, you may unbind her hands as you did her feet. She will be secured to the altar when the time comes. There will be no option but to finish the sacrificial obligation she has promised."

With this Taylor's eyes narrowed and she screamed out, "What obligation?! What promise? I didn't promise to do any of this! You are making this all up so you can justify whatever it is you think you are doing!" She buried her face in Gail's neck as she clung to her mother for support.

"Oh, but you did, Taylor Wright. You gave me your word that you would share in the cause to rid the world of wrongdoers, to help in the final destiny, to bring justice to all, and move into the spiritual afterworld with me."

Taylor started choking on words. "Wha . . . what, Carlos? Oh my God, why? This was not what you made me believe. This is all a lie. You never said anything about murder or sacrificing humans. You lied to me."

"You and your family came to me. You got in the car, and you are now here. This is your fate. Liag saw it all in a vision. He told me this was how it would unfold. If it were not supposed to be, why did it all happen exactly as he said? It was not I who lied, Taylor. You chose not to see the truth." With that Carlos left the hysterical girl to be soothed by her mother. He closed the door and locked it. He went to find Liag and to officially begin the ceremony. The drummers would signify the beginning of the ritual that would initiate the optimism of the future and, as Liag had so often spoken of, expose the misconduct of the world, avenging it in a swift and final manner.

CHAPTER 51

AMANDA REACHED THE OPPOSITE SIDE OF THE PERIMETER OF THE COMPOUND IN NO TIME. She had jogged almost all the way and was breathing heavily but quietly as she waited for Jake. She had seen at least one other guard closer to the buildings on her way around. She was pretty sure she was at the right spot and was concerned because Jake, who was swifter than she was, should have been there already. After two minutes, she was ready to break radio silence when a hand shot out and quickly grabbed her face, covering her mouth and nose. She couldn't breathe. Jake quickly turned her around, put his finger to his lips, and pointed out a robed man carrying an assault rifle passing only ten feet in front of her, doing his rounds.

Once the man was a good distance away, Jake mouthed, "Sorry."

Amanda composed herself and then whispered, "What happened? You're late."

Jake motioned toward the guard. "He was pretty deep in. I had to hold back or engage. I chose to hold back because at this point anything could set these guys off, and for all we know they would make a clean sweep of the situation; we might get out, but nobody else would."

She knew he was right, and she knew she had to tell him what she had seen in her vision. She didn't know if it was a good time but also didn't know if there ever would be a good time during this mission, so she grabbed his arm and looked into his eyes. "Keith is dead." She didn't know how else to put it. Jake looked torn. She knew he had difficulty believing without seeing, and she didn't blame him for that, but to his credit he just nodded and said, "Let's go, then. We don't want to lose anyone else."

Amanda took the lead. She had better eyes, and Jake had better reflexes in case someone snuck up from behind. Since the oval building was the largest of the bunch and on higher ground, they assumed there was something going down there. They moved around the building but couldn't see any openings on the back side. They did see a small bulge jutting out of the round side on the back, and at the top of that hump was a small round hole, like a window, probably to let air into the small area beneath.

"What do you make of that?" Amanda nodded toward the small addition on the building.

"I'm guessing some kind of small offshoot to the main area. Not sure if you noticed, but the dome roof is flat on top. I am going to climb a tree to get a better look. I'll need you to watch for me in case one of our gun-happy monks comes along."

"No problem." Amanda watched as Jake shimmied up a tree about five yards back of where she kept watch. He reminded her of the coconut-tree climbers in Ko Olina who, in a matter of seconds, were able to climb a tree, cut down a bunch of king coconuts, slide down, slice one open, and offer you the sweet juice to guzzle on a hot day. Suddenly Amanda wished she was back at their condo in Oahu rather than risking their lives on another crazy mission. But then she remembered all those summers watching Taylor grow up, playing with the kids on the Sea-Doos, and wakeboarding. They had no choice but to try to save her, without a doubt.

Amanda suddenly felt the presence of something ominous and ducked just as the butt end of a rifle struck at her head. She rolled and grabbed for her knife strapped to the side of her boot. When she looked up the hooded figure was swinging the rifle around, no doubt to fill her full of lead and alert the entire world of their attempted rescue when, as if by magic, the hooded villain was lifted right off the ground. In his surprise he let the gun drop and Amanda lunged for it and kicked it out of reach. The sentry started clawing at the arm wrapped around his neck, so Amanda kicked him hard in the groin, causing him to pull his knees close to his chest in agonizing pain, but he was unable to make more than a gurgling sound.

Behind him, Jake held tight as the hood fell down, revealing a purple face. The man's eyes rolled back as he went limp in Jake's arm. The man wasn't that tall, but Amanda was impressed that Jake, at barely five foot eleven, was able to lift him right off the ground.

Amanda immediately checked the man's pulse. He was alive, but she was pretty sure he wouldn't be feeling too great when he came around. She removed the man's robe, duct-taped his hands and feet, and placed another piece over his mouth. Then Jake dragged him about a hundred feet back into the jungle and lay him down behind some brush. At least he wouldn't get a sunburn. Jake noted the GPS coordinates so the authorities could find him. Amanda and Jake didn't want to kill anyone and always felt it was better for the bad guys to serve time in prison for their crimes than get the easy way out through death.

"Well, I was right," Jake said after returning from depositing the gunman. "No roof, just a big round opening to the sky."

"Makes sense," Amanda remarked. "What we are dealing with is some sort of voodoo rite and ceremonial ritual. There was the talk of voodoo in the e-mails, the mask on the tree marking the territory, and the hooded priests."

"OK, so what does that have to do with the roof, or should I say the lack of roof, on this building?"

"It is probably a ceremonial room designed for the ritual offerings associated with whatever high spirits these guys are worshipping. Generally, voodoo is a good religion." Jake looked surprised. "Its roots are African, but as slaves were imported to Haiti, the religion came too. Haitian voodoo is more colorful, but it all boils down to appeasing certain houses of spirits. They all require a blood sacrifice, but which family of spirits you worship depends on how extreme your ceremonies are. There are hot spirits and cool spirits, and the hot ones generally have a more explicit way of dealing with evil. There tends to be a funnel of sorts that channels the spirits. It can be an opening in a jungle canopy or a hole in a hut roof. I am no expert, but it seems that all things are pointing to a convoluted mix of these different beliefs."

"OK, so how does that help us?" Jake inquired.

"It doesn't." Amanda suddenly brightened. "How tall do you figure that guy back there is?"

Jake smiled. "Not much shorter than me. In fact, we're almost the same height." Then he held out the robe he had pulled off the gunman.

"That's what I thought." She grinned and handed the M16 to Jake.

CHAPTER 52

DETECTIVE TAO WAS CONTEMPLATING BREAKFAST WHEN THE
PHONE RANG.

"Tao here."

"Hey, buddy," Tony's bold voice on the other end blared through the
receiver. "Got something interesting here. Not sure how much you know
about these two Canucks."

"Not a lot. Why don't you fill me in?"

"Well, first of all, Wright and Stevens were partners on the force for a
lot of years. Then there was this rookie that Wright had to assist—you know,
train up. Well, it was some hot Spanish chick, and he ended up having an
affair. Things turned ugly. Wright's wife left him and hooked up with Stevens. That's the way it went down."

"OK, besides all the smut, anything else interesting that could connect
these guys? Anything about Carlos or voodoo or this case?'

"Hey, man, don't get edgy. You asked for help. I am doing what I can
to get you some."

"Sorry, Tony. This case is driving me crazy. I have three, no, actually five
innocent people out there that I am responsible for, and I have nothing."

"Well, that's not exactly true. You do have something." Tony's voice
took on a hushed tone. "Listen, man, some people could get into big trouble,

some good guys, so whatever I tell you now is on the QT. Use it for whatever it's worth, but you didn't get it from me, right?"

"Right." Tao was all ears now.

"This Bernie Wright fellow worked on a few things with my buddy in Edmonton, a few domestics. After his wife left I guess they kind of kept him on some easy shit. They said he got depressed—you know, drinking a lot, not leaving his house much, and not focusing on cases. He has a sister in Arkansas and spent a lot of time down there. Anyway, the guy was in a bad way for some time. He even got hooked on some anti-anxiety pills and got set up with some cops in Arkansas. They 'helped' him out, if you know what I mean. He made frequent trips down there and got hooked up through some of the guys who had connections with the inmates at FCI Forrest City Pen."

"OK, Tony, so the guy was buying. He had formed a habit because he was in a bad way. We've seen this movie before. What's the deal?"

"That's the deal, Ron. He apparently started coming in to visit the same guy often enough for some of the guards to notice, a guy by the name of Durrant."

"Yeah and . . . " Detective Tao was getting impatient.

"Yeah and," Tony continued, "Durrant, first name Carlos."

CHAPTER 53

THE SUDDEN SOUND OF THE DRUMS STARTLED TAYLOR. Huddled in the corner of the room, she and Gail were terrified by the dark and penetrating rhythmic beat. Taylor was now wearing the white dress, her clothes in a heap next to her. Gail never wore a watch. She listened intently to the drums for a few minutes, then sighed. "Wonder how long it's been." Taylor moved to the pile of clothes and pulled out her cell phone. Gail's eyes widened. "Honey, what are you doing with that? Didn't they take it from you?"

"Nope. Guess they didn't think it would matter out here. There is no reception anyway, and I don't think they were planning on letting me escape. Either that or they couldn't find it; it was in my lower cargo pocket in my pants, and it's really small."

"Does it have the time?"

"Yep, let me turn it on. I shut it down 'cause I wanted to conserve the battery—you know, to text Dad if we escaped and got into coverage." When the phone powered up, the time and date showed January 2, 2011, 11:45 a.m. "Mom, we're not gonna get out of this, are we?" she asked.

Gail was heartbroken. She didn't know what to tell her. Bernie was their only hope, but he would have been there by now if he had any clue as to their whereabouts. All she could do was try to take their minds off the inevitable. "Remember when we went to Disney World in Florida and you got lost, or thought you did but really we were following you? You wanted to be all independent, but when you lost sight of us for even a few minutes, you got scared. I remember seeing your face, and even though your dad wanted to hold back so you could learn a lesson, I just didn't have the heart. I ran over to you and picked you up and smothered you with kisses and everything was OK."

"Yeah, I still remember that. It was the time we went on that Tower of Terror and I peed my pants," Taylor admitted. She was still embarrassed about that all these years later.

"Well," continued Gail, "I really wish I could just pick you up and smother you with kisses and everything could be fixed. But I can't this time, Taylor." Her eyes filled with tears and Taylor nodded. Now it was her turn to embrace her mom and smooth down her hair and soothe her with soft hushes. It was almost as if they had formed a new bond, one that would keep them strong enough to endure whatever happened next.

They stayed that way for what felt like a very long time. It had to be much longer than the hour that was given to them. They worried about what would happen next. The sound of the drums beat in time with the sound of Taylor's heart. She was lulled into a dream state, thinking about Disney World and walking holding her mom's hand, laughing at all the characters dancing by. There was Cinderella, Nemo, and—she opened her eyes slightly—yes, Goofy, right in front of her in the doorway. Just then the door of the small room creaked open and Carlos entered, sword swinging dangerously at his side.

CHAPTER 54

"Great, when does the chanting start?" Jake's sarcasm was heavy when he heard the drums. Dressed in the robe that was removed from the sentry, Jake complimented Amanda's handiwork. "I think he's gonna be out for a while, and when he wakes up, he ain't going anywhere. Nice job with the duct tape back there."

"That's my specialty," Amanda said and smirked. "OK, so the plan is easy: you go and start your guard duties." Amanda was curious about how long they had wasted just trying to get to the compound. It seemed like all morning, and when she checked her watch she found she was right. It was getting close to noon and the bright sunshine made it amazingly hot. "I am going to try to scramble around and get some bearings on the round room. If you can, try to make it to the helicopter to radio for help first. At least then we'd know the cavalry was on its way." Then she stroked Jake's chin. "Listen, honey, you know how to fly; I don't. If things get hairy and it looks like nobody's getting out of this one, I want you to promise me that, given the opportunity, you will get in that chopper and go."

"Sure thing, princess. I'll be on it like a fat kid on a cookie." Amanda knew Jake was just telling her what she wanted to hear, and that bothered her more than anything because he had a sure way out that he wasn't going to use, and it was her fault he was here in the first place.

"OK, then at least promise me you won't get killed, because you are our one and only ride out of here."

"I give you my word. I promise I won't get killed. I swear on my life." He smiled and kissed her forehead.

"Very funny." She gave him the signal for radio silence, for now anyway. She headed out toward the building, grabbing the pack on her way, and he swung the M16 onto his shoulder and headed out straight into the middle of the action, walking calmly and slowly toward the Bell 206. He almost started humming to the beat of the drums. They seemed to come from all sides of the mud buildings. *I hope they don't have that many musically talented gunmen*, Jake thought as he rounded the far side of the building.

"Oh, she's a beauty," he sarcastically remarked under his breath. "Someone has not been taking good care of you, little bird," Jake said as he approached the helicopter. He took a sweeping glance to ensure that nobody was around and then peered in through the window. *Yes! There is a radio and GPS*, he thought to himself, *and of course there should be an emergency locator transmitter.* He wasn't sure what he was going to find. It seemed someone had stripped everything out of the bird. *Probably to carry more gear*, he thought. The accommodations were a bit less than he had expected in this 206, which was one of Jake's favorite helicopters. He noticed the Bell was properly tied down but wasn't sure if the door was locked. Jake slowly turned the handle of the pilot-side door and it popped open easily. He was about to climb in when he noticed something in his peripheral vision. About fifty yards away, he could barely make out Amanda being pushed forward in a full nelson by one of the armed guards. She didn't have the pack anymore. She must have managed to store it somewhere prior to getting caught. *What the heck?* he thought. *She normally can feel something coming a mile away. What happened?* Jake had a lump in his throat. He could stay as cool as a cucumber in almost any situation, except when it came to Amanda.

He looked up just in time to see the robed figure pull her other arm behind her, ripping the surgical tape from her arm as he tied it roughly with nylon rope, causing the wound to begin bleeding again. He pushed her toward the front opening in the oval building. Jake felt a surge of rage and then had to talk himself down. He knew getting upset and storming the place by himself wouldn't help. He could set the emergency locator transmitter off right then, but before he had a chance another sentry came out of nowhere. Jake had to duck down behind the Bell in order not to be seen, and of course the sentry was headed directly toward him. *No time to set it off now*, he thought as he inched away from the helicopter and the path of the oncoming sentry.

He decided to retrace Amanda's route to find the pack of supplies. He knew he would need them if he were to have any chance of getting everyone out alive.

CHAPTER 55

AMANDA COULDN'T BELIEVE IT. She had stashed her bag about fifty feet back in order to make herself lighter and less noisy as she approached the building. She had let her guard down, worrying about Jake, that he was not going to use the helicopter for himself. She was pondering how she could somehow change his mind if she were to get nabbed while stealthily moving along when a large hand wrenched her face from behind, almost snapping her neck. She was flipped onto her stomach, and a heavy knee dug deep into the middle of her back. She could not turn her head enough to see her assailant, but she had no doubt that whoever it was had been military-trained and was very stealthy. The man jerked her arm behind her back and yanked her to a standing position by the back of her shirt. The way he pulled her around with such ease, she could tell the man was well built. Lifting her was probably like nothing more than lifting the free weights he curled on a regular basis. Amanda cursed under her breath for allowing herself to get caught.

"Quiet." The man spoke in a deep voice, slapping the back of her head hard. She winced from the pain, and he roughly pushed her forward toward the oval building, twisting her arm behind her back so that she was forced to comply.

Amanda walked steadily forward. *Well, at least we're going where I was headed in the first place*, she thought. While they were in the open area in front of the building, she scanned the area, looking for Jake. She tried not to be obvious so her captor would not know she had an accomplice. When she noticed the Bell ahead to her left she hoped to see Jake, but he wasn't there. Her eyes watered with tears as her heart felt Jake's eyes on her, and she could sense his rage throughout her entire body. *I hope he doesn't do anything stupid*, she thought. She knew Jake, even in all his fury, would think of a way to get them out, so she moved along, formulating in her mind a plan to get out of this mess, if they were given the chance.

CHAPTER 56

DETECTIVE TAO FRANTICALLY GOT HIS PAPERWORK PROCESSED
FOR THE HELICOPTER AND A PILOT TO FLY HIM TO THE INTERIOR OF
THE ISLAND. It had taken him all morning, and since he was working on a
hunch, he told the flight coordinator that he was going on a routine scouting mission. He was grateful for the information Tony had supplied him
with, but knew he wouldn't be able to use any of it to get assistance. He was
definitely on his own for this one.

He had his standard-issue Smith & Wesson and a few cartridges. He
was always prepared but also hoped he wouldn't have to use it. He drove to
meet the pilot at the Hilo airport. His name was Jonah Riley Samson, but
everyone called him J.R., and he was an excellent bush pilot. He had spent
the majority of his flying days with the 101st Airborne Division and then,
after his last tour during the Persian Gulf War, when he was part of opera-
tion Desert Storm, he spent some time fighting forest fires in the Canadian
Rockies. When his girlfriend in Vancouver fell in love with her lesbian mas-
sage therapist, Kate, his ego couldn't take it and he moved to the islands to
find himself and figure things out.

J.R. loved the sand and surf and the long, lazy days of perfect weather.
He didn't mind the occasional hurricanes, but he missed his time flying a
whirlybird in the mountains. He signed up with the police force to do special missions in Hawaii. J.R. worked with all the teams on all the islands.

Helping the police was kind of therapeutic for him, whether it was finding lost hikers or responding to major emergencies. He felt like it was a small contribution, but it kept him sane, and that was why he stayed involved.

"J.R., it's been a while." Tao smiled as he shook the pilot's hand.

"It's a good day for a scouting mission, huh?" said J.R.

"Well, it might not be as routine as I made out. Truth be known, this one might get a bit dangerous. It's a big, ugly case with hair on it. It involves a fifteen-year-old girl." J.R. perked up. He had seen a lot of abuse of teenage girls and younger during his tour, and he hated all of it. "I thought that would get your attention. Sorry for not giving you more information up front, but you know how it is trying to get through the red tape."

"What's the deal? Are we tactically set up or is this a fly-by-the-seat-of-our-pants-style mission?"

Tao looked away for a few seconds, then he stared directly into the eyes of the pilot. "I would say fly-by-the-seat-of-our-pants, but I am not sure we even have the pants, if you know what I mean."

"Been there, tackled that. Didn't write the book, but I should have." J.R. smirked. "Well, giddy up. You can fill me in on those details you don't have on the flight over."

CHAPTER 57

JAKE RETRACED THE ROUTE HE KNEW AMANDA WOULD MOST LIKELY HAVE TAKEN. He could see where the struggle had been and where she was most likely taken down by the guard. Beads of sweat streamed down Jake's face. He blinked them away as he moved backward, stepping gingerly to ensure he didn't miss anything. He could clearly make out her tracks, but about forty-five feet back he started to panic, thinking he was wasting his time looking for a pack when Amanda was in danger. The sun was hot, but Jake noticed that it had moved quite a bit. Time was passing. He checked his Daytona; it was now just after 3:00 p.m. He had to get them out before dark or it would be nearly impossible. He was about to give up on the pack when he saw a small mound covered in the same manner as he had covered the climbing gear on the cliff. "And she thinks I do a lousy camouflage job," he whispered to himself. Jake quickly cleared the dirt and leaves and pulled the pack out from under it. He put it on under the robe and started back toward the building, feeling more confident. Jake moved toward the back of the building opposite to the opening that Amanda had been pushed through. He tried to block the images in his mind of the large figure manhandling her and her arm bleeding. He knew that she sensed him and felt that he had seen her. He only hoped that she could hold out until he got to her.

Jake was furious that Amanda was in the hands of these animals. She was always doing things to help everyone else, and this was where it got her.

He was determined to rescue her if it was the last thing he did on this planet. To hell with everyone else. *If we get out of this one*, he thought, *we are retiring*. He then imagined the fight he would get from Amanda. He pictured her standing with her hands on her hips, shaking her head from side to side, saying, "Oh no, Jake, *you* may be retiring, but . . ." The thought of his spunky little girl helped put his mind at ease just a little bit. At that moment he had no doubt she would somehow escape, with or without his help, although he preferred to be the one to save her. However, right now he would take a win no matter how it happened.

Jake quickly worked his way back toward the compound and tried to find an alternate entry. At the back of the building he noticed that, besides the gaping hole at the top, there was a smaller hole in the alcove extending off the back. *Well, looks like that may be the only other way in*, he thought, unless he wanted to drop down like a spider right through the center of the building, exposing himself to the entire room. It worked for Tom Cruise in *Mission: Impossible*, but Jake didn't think it would work for him. He pulled a thin climbing rope from his pack and attached a small, three-prong hook to it. He hoped that he would be able to catch the hook on the inside wall well enough to hold his hundred and ninety-seven pounds. *Well, here goes nothing*, he thought as he flung the rope skillfully through the window.

CHAPTER 58

"It's time." The words reverberated off the walls of the small room. Taylor, now dressed in the white ceremonial gown, cast her eyes back down to the floor. She hated the sight of Carlos and his ugly, tattooed face. The thought that she had done this to her family was driving her insane. Now the time had come, and there was nothing she could do about it. She felt her mother's strong arm around her shoulders as they slowly moved out of the alcove into the hall. She suddenly felt a sense of relief. Maybe this was for the best. Her dad wasn't coming to save them, and if she was to be sacrificed first, at least she would not be around to watch what happened to her mom.

Taylor had not thought about Keith since the gunshot. She never did really like him, but her mom seemed to find some kind of solace from being with him, so Taylor put up with him. She had a feeling the gunshot she heard earlier was for Keith, and, really, it didn't matter all that much. They would all be dead soon. She felt bad for her mom, who would most likely have to watch whatever was about to happen to her. She had heard so many times how the worst thing that can happen to a parent is to have a child precede them in death. Taylor wondered how much worse it would be to have your child precede you in a ritual sacrifice. She thought about her dad again, how he got drunk after the separation from Mom. Maybe he didn't want to save them. Maybe he thought they deserved to be kidnapped. She quickly put the thought out of her mind. She knew her dad loved her. How could he possibly know where they were and not save them? Obviously the local police hadn't tracked them down, so how could her dad, thousands of miles away, ever have a chance of saving them? The tears rolled down her cheeks and dripped off her chin, staining the pretty white dress. Taylor didn't openly break down; she only let her tears fall for all the days in her young life she would miss with her friends and her family. And for all the things she had taken for granted, like her home and safety and, most of all, for the stupid mistake of getting involved with a stranger online.

CHAPTER 59

JAKE WATCHED AS THE ROPE AND HOOK LANDED FIRMLY THROUGH
THE OPENING WITH A THUD. He gave the rope a couple of very strong
tugs. It seemed to have caught. He moved in toward the wall and gripped
the rope, steadying one foot, then the other, against the side of the building.
He moved slowly up toward the opening. Although the rope seemed to be
holding, it seemed like the hook was connected to only the dirt wall on the
other side of the window and could easily start sliding up through the dirt
and come hurling back down toward him. He could end up falling fifteen
feet or so and get a hook in the eye.

He quickly took off the robe and put the pack on. He kept an eye out
for signs of the hooded guards, although there could be more inside. They
had seen only four guards around the perimeter. One was disposed of, and
one had dragged Amanda into the building. Amanda would have sensed if
there were more than that. That left two guards, and Jake hoped they stayed
on the front side of the building, where they were stationed earlier. He wondered if the drummers were also armed. As if reacting to his thoughts, the
drumming picked up speed, sounding like a racing heartbeat. Jake realized
his heart was racing to the beat of the drums, and he had an ominous feeling. To his far right, he could just make out the tail of the helicopter. If only
he had Amanda with him he would be out of there in a flash. But he wasn't
going anywhere without her. He was about six feet up the wall and about

to take the next step when he felt a sharp pain against his side. A strong arm reached around his neck and tightened until he started to see flashes in front of his eyes. He was blacking out as the large, hooded guard dragged him down the rope by the neck. Jake stopped struggling to keep the knife from digging deeper into his side, and he gasped desperately for air on the way down. Just as his feet struck the ground, Jake bit into the forearm of the guard as hard as he could. He tasted blood, and the man loosened his grip around his throat. It was just enough for Jake to twist away, losing the pack off his back, and grab the man's hand holding the knife. Face to face with his assailant, Jake was about half a foot shorter. He jumped straight up and butted the man's face hard with the top of his head. The man yelped and released Jake as blood sprayed from his broken nose. Jake knew better than to allow the brute time to recover, because once his adrenalin kicked in, the big man would snap him like a twig. Jake punched him twice in the face with quick jabs. The guard staggered with one hand up against his face and swung the knife toward Jake with his other hand. Jake grabbed the guard's wrist, which felt like a solid tree branch, and bent it backward while throwing a quick knee directly into the man's groin. Falling to his knees, the guard let go of his nose and pulled Jake down by the front of his shirt, partially ripping the fabric. Jake twisted the guard's wrist as they both fell to the ground. The knife fell between them. Jake rolled away from the guard, leaving a large part of his shirt in the man's grasp. He managed to stand just as the guard reached over, snagged the knife, and, still on his knees, lunged toward Jake, who stepped down hard on the guard's hand and then spun around, kicking the man square in the face. Blood and teeth flew through the air, but the man did not go down. Jake kicked the knife about six feet away and quickly picked up the pack and ripped open the front zipper, pulling out one of Amanda's syringes that contained propofol. He threw the pack aside just as the guard rushed him, pinning him against the side of the building. Jake couldn't move. In his left hand he held the needle tight, but the man was crushing him against the building. He felt like his ribs were about to give way. He looked up, and the bloodied face grinned back with broken teeth and a crooked nose. The man moved his right arm across Jake's body to the opposite side and up the side of Jake's face. Jake knew he was going to try to snap his neck in one quick motion. As the guard tried to snake his arm around Jake's head, Jake strained his neck away and slowly twisted his left hand, placing his thumb on the needle plunger and edging his wrist into an uncomfortable but necessary position so he could push the needle into the man's thigh while still trying to keep the large man's open hand away from his neck. As he did this, the man flinched for a second, then looked down at his thigh like he had been bitten by a mosquito. Jake watched as the guard's eyes slowly started to glaze over, and he loosened his grip. Jake knew it was just enough propofol to render the man unconscious for a few hours. He hoped that was all he and Amanda would need. He understood the reason behind having propofol, as Amanda explained. No reason to kill a rhino, just put him under, make him helpless. The man slid down Jake's body into a very large pile at his feet. Jake kicked the man away. "And then there was one," he said, referencing the only guard left on the perimeter, "and if I'm lucky I will not have the pleasure of meeting him." Jake grabbed the pack and his gun and picked up the guard's knife before turning back to the rope still dangling down the wall.

CHAPTER 60

AMANDA WAS FACEDOWN IN THE DIRT. All she could see were the feet of the guard who had dragged her into the room and thrown her down. He had tied her hands behind her back and her feet together. She was pretty much immobile and had been that way for some time. *Ugh*, she thought as she tried to move. She did not want to become stiff, especially if she had to move quickly at some point. It had been at least thirty minutes since she had been brought into the room. She figured it was going on 4:00 p.m. *Where the hell was Jake?* Then she sensed that she was not alone in the room with the guard. There was someone else, a familiar presence, but she couldn't quite place it. She could hear shuffling somewhere off to her left, and just as she was wondering where Gail and Taylor might be, she sensed that they were there.

She lifted her head up as far as she was able and noticed shadows, and then she saw Taylor and Gail followed by a giant, dark figure. Suddenly she was pulled up by the back of her shirt into a sitting position on the floor. Gail gasped when she recognized Amanda with her arm bleeding, dirty and tied up in the corner.

Amanda's arm was stinging, and she could feel blood trickling down and knew there was grit and dirt inside the cut from all the struggling. She imagined it would be nicely infected in the next few hours. She concentrated her efforts on clearing her mind, as her ability to sense things was dulled when she was stressed or under pressure. She could feel the presence of those around her, but she had a hard time bringing their fears and thoughts into focus. They were clamoring in her head. She could feel Taylor's helplessness—she looked like she was in a trance. *She has given up*, Amanda thought. She could sense Gail was randomly running through scenarios of escape. Amanda knew Gail was willing to sacrifice herself if she had to. The creepiest thing was that Amanda could feel someone else nearby, someone she knew or who knew her, but they were not on the same team. Amanda couldn't quite figure it out. A quick count in her head told her there were still two guards outside; one inside; the large, tall, creepy figure with Gail and Taylor; and someone else. She thought that she had to be getting cross signals from Gail or Taylor, as the presence seemed way too familiar to her. If Jake was there, her feelings would be intensely good. She could feel that he was close by but not yet in their room. The light coming in from the roof was starting to dim, making it difficult to see who and where everyone was. Shadows in the corners looked like guards. The drumming was at a fever pitch and remarkably loud. She scanned the roof of the building and noticed small speakers mounted strategically in the circular area. *Oh, that is where the drums are coming from*, she thought. *So there isn't a full band of drummers hiding behind door number one.* That was a good thing. Jake was very capable, but even he couldn't take on ten armed men all at once. Four or five was a stretch, but he'd still have a good chance.

Amanda focused, trying to foresee an outcome. If she could see a bit of the future, or even the past, she might have a psychological advantage. The tall, dark figure moved from behind the two women to the center of the room. The guard who had caught Amanda walked up behind Gail and Taylor to ensure that they didn't try to escape. Amanda did not see anything but a dark hallway behind them and figured the only way out was through the small, round window she and Jake had seen.

Amanda noticed that the tall man had crossed to the center of the room, where the late-afternoon sun shone down. She gasped as the shadows moving up and down his face and neck turned into snakes, slithering in the sunlight. It took her mind a minute to register that they were tattoos as the man turned away from the sunlight for a moment.

"Liag, it is time." From the dark corner a much smaller figure came out, almost as if coming out of the wall itself, wearing the same long robe and hood as the guards. The figure did not speak. He just nodded at the tall one. The man with the dancing snake face walked over to Taylor and took her arm. The piercing shriek coming from Gail's lips made Amanda's heart jump. Gail lunged forward to try to stop the man from taking her daughter, but the armed guard grabbed a handful of her hair and held her back with little effort.

Gail's shrieks continued as she pleaded for her daughter's life, asking that she be the one sacrificed and to let her daughter go. Amanda watched intensely as they made Taylor lie on the altar and bound her wrists and ankles on the sides. *What is taking Jake so long?* Amanda screamed in her head. She started to worry that he wasn't coming at all.

CHAPTER 61

JAKE HEARD THE HEART-WRENCHING CRIES OF GAIL PLEADING FOR THE LIFE OF HER DAUGHTER AND QUICKLY TOOK OUT HIS GLOCK. He only hoped he was not too late and that there weren't twenty armed guards waiting for him in that circular room. The beating drums continued through Gail's wailing, and he hoped that Amanda could feel his presence and would be able to distract the group so that he could make the best of his entrance. He snuck along close to the wall, hoping nobody would come strolling down the hallway to the little room. It was getting late in the afternoon and soon the room would be dark, which was both an advantage and a disadvantage. If he could get a good glimpse of the room, he would be able to make a plan, but he knew he was running out of time. Silently he crept down the hall closer to the entrance to the room. He could barely make out the back of the guard who had nabbed Amanda earlier. *OK*, Jake thought, *I will have to take out this guy first and then whoever is left in that room.* He slowly got down on all fours and then flat on his stomach and inched his way closer to the opening. He could just make out the figures in what remained of the late-afternoon sun streaming in through the roof. He could make out a small blonde head on the long stone altar in the middle of the room. He saw the back of a tall bald man who had an amazingly long sword attached to the belt tied around his robe. Jake poked his head slowly around the corner. Scanning the entire room, he could make out the feet of another person on the opposite side of the altar. On her knees in between the bald man and the guard closest to Jake was Gail. Her face was in her hands and she was sobbing uncontrollably. Jake knew he didn't have time to feel sorry for anyone at the moment. He had to concentrate. He felt Amanda's eyes on him way before he actually saw her. She stared directly at him then turned quickly the other way. He knew it was nearly impossible for her to actually see him in the dim room, especially while he lay flat on the floor in the dark hallway, but he knew that she sensed he was there, and that was a good thing. *Now what will she do next?* he wondered as he aimed the gun carefully at the leg of the guard in front of him.

CHAPTER 62

TAYLOR TRIED TO TUNE OUT HER MOTHER'S CRIES. Tears streamed down the sides of her face as she lay still on the cold altar. She knew that there was nothing she could do to change what was happening and the best thing to hope for was a quick end to it all. She had no idea what type of ceremony this could be. She remembered Carlos talking about sacrifices done to please spirits or gods and some that were an offering to gain favor when you passed into the spiritual world. She never imagined that *he* would be doing any sacrificing. He had talked about the other world and spiritual things and heaven and preparing for when that time came. Taylor had been more or less infatuated with Carlos. He seemed so deep and sincere in his e-mails. He was a committed soul, something she didn't run across much in her high-school circles. She never really paid much attention to his rants. She never thought that his invitation for them to meet would end in her death and the death of her mother. For the first time since she had walked in the room like a zombie, Taylor realized it was Amanda Bannon who was sitting on the floor to her right, hands and feet tied. *What's Amanda doing here?* she thought. Taylor suddenly jerked up as far as the ropes would allow her. "Amanda!" she cried. "You're here! My dad must know. He must have called you. Is he coming?" Taylor spat the words out almost hysterically, trying to turn her head as far around as possible to see Amanda. She needed to know Amanda was really there and she wasn't just imagining things.

"Taylor," Amanda replied in as soothing a voice as she could muster. "Stay calm. It's OK. Just relax and try to conserve your energy." She said this as slowly as she could, hoping Taylor would understand she needed to rest in case they had to move fast once Jake made the rescue attempt.

"But does my dad know?" Taylor's question was so quiet and sad that Amanda almost broke down herself.

She was about to answer when the large man with the snake tattoos spoke in a loud, deep voice: "Quiet! The ceremony must begin at sunset, Liag. We cannot wait much longer. I will light the candles." With that he struck a match and started going around the room to the little tables set up with the white flowers and candles, slowly lighting each one, chanting unrecognizable words under his breath.

Taylor broke in: "Whatever you are doing, Carlos, it won't work."

So this is Carlos, Amanda thought. *Hmmm, not exactly what Gail and Bernie would have wanted for a son-in-law.*

"My dad will be here any minute with a truckload of police. If Amanda found us, then my dad will know. And if I'm dead when he gets here, he will personally tear you apart!"

Carlos crossed the room so quickly it startled Amanda. He swiftly unsheathed his sword as he neared the altar. Gail let out a bloodcurdling scream. Amanda tried to think of a way to stop Carlos. She felt completely helpless. Where was Jake? Suddenly, the dark figure in the corner stepped out and put up his hand. Carlos stopped.

"Liag, it is time. We cannot wait. We will miss the time of sacrifice. The gods will not be pleased."

The hooded figure walked up to Carlos and put his hand on his shoulder. Carlos bent down as the man whispered in his ear. The drums continued to beat through the speakers, and Amanda's arm was now burning with irritation and her head pounded. She was very warm and figured she must have a fever from the infection in her arm. She watched as Carlos seemed to be shaking his head faster and faster, and then a slow moan started from his lips. "Nooooo," he was saying over and over. The hooded man continued to whisper in a more urgent manner. Carlos continued to shake his head and then fell to his knees.

What is going on? Amanda wondered. *Whatever it is, this is about the best time as any to go for it. Whatever is transpiring between those two is unexpected,* she thought. *So might as well go along with the unexpected theme.* With that she slowly slid her tied legs under her and tried to stand up. She fell over with a small thud. The guard behind Gail looked her way, but seeing her lying still, he looked back over at the ensuing conversation between Carlos and Liag. Amanda watched the guard and then looked down at Gail. Suddenly, as if someone took a pen and drew it for her, the name Gail was floating in front of her eyes. *Great, now I'm hallucinating. Must be the fever,* Amanda thought, but it was her intuition kicking into high gear. She had been thinking about the name Liag before. She scratched it with her foot in the dirt on the ground in front of her, and it became immediately apparent: *Liag* was *Gail* spelled backward.

CHAPTER 63

JAKE DIDN'T GET IT. The big man was on his knees, and it looked like he was upset or something. He had heard Taylor call him Carlos, and of course it was. *Who else could it be, right? But who is the other dude, and what kind of power does he have over that giant ape?* Jake thought. He had seen Amanda try to stand and fall and was hoping she would distract them. But what was she doing now, writing something in the dirt with her foot? Jake stared at her quizzically. *What the heck is she doing? This is no time to be playing Xs and Os,* he thought. When she looked up from her scribbling, she was as white as a ghost. Whatever it was, it wasn't good. She looked in his direction and nodded. That was the sign; she was going to make her move.

Jake watched as Amanda in one heaving action jumped to her feet. The guard near Gail immediately aimed his semi automatic in Amanda's direction as he walked quickly toward her. Amanda was swaying as she tried to stand. This caught the attention of Liag, who turned to see what was going on. Carlos suddenly stood. "Liag, you will not stop this. This is even greater than you. We have worked for years to get to this stage. You will not stop me from getting what is rightfully mine. I will sacrifice the girl."

Jake could not wait a second longer. Either Amanda or Taylor would die in the next five minutes if he didn't act now. He scrambled to his feet and walked into the room, gun pointed directly at the back of Carlos's head. "I don't think we want to do a ritual killing today, Carlos."

Carlos spun around to see Jake standing there, gun in hand, cocked and ready to shoot. Liag slowly pulled his gun from beneath his robe and held it carefully at his side. The guard who was heading toward Amanda turned and aimed his gun at Jake. "I don't think you want to do that or I will load one right through your friend Carlos's head. I'm a darn good shot, but if you want to take a chance, go for it." The guard hesitated and looked over at Carlos and Liag.

"Shoot him," Carlos said. As the words were coming out of Carlos's mouth, Amanda lunged forward, crashing into the back of the guard and sending him flying toward Jake.

As the guard flew forward he let off a round in Jake's direction. At the same time Jake pulled his trigger.

One of the guard's bullets hit the gun right out of Jake's hand while another struck his left leg just above the kneecap, sending him to the ground bleeding.

Amanda hit the dirt face-first. *That's gonna leave a mark*, she thought. She didn't have a chance to see what happened; she only heard a loud bang and then heard Gail shriek, "Oh my God, Jake." Amanda had a sinking feeling, but she would know right away if Jake were dead. She could see the gunman's feet just a few feet away, not moving. *Good*, she thought as dizziness swept over her. She could hear a loud roar, almost inhuman, and she turned her head to see Liag and Carlos in a tight embrace across the room behind the altar. She thought she was imagining it when she felt her arms and feet being cut free.

CHAPTER 64

GAIL HAD USED JAKE'S KNIFE TO CUT THROUGH THE ROPES THAT BOUND AMANDA'S HANDS AND FEET. Jake had managed to throw the knife over to Gail after shooting the guard. Gail's first thought was to free Taylor, but she didn't think that could happen with Carlos and Liag right by the altar. Jake was trying to regain strength in his leg and was half walking, half crawling toward his gun, which had flown a good distance away from him. It now lay between the two fighting men and the wall. He wasn't sure what was going on, but it seemed there was some kind of dispute, and he didn't want to get in their way. He hoped Amanda could get Gail and Taylor out of there while he held those two off, or finished them off, or better yet, while they finished each other off.

Gail untied Amanda and quickly moved toward the altar. "Gail, no!" Amanda whispered as loud as she dared. "They will kill you."

Gail turned on Amanda. "It's not your daughter up there, is it, Amanda? You can sit here and watch, but I won't."

Oh God, Amanda thought as she kept glancing up at Gail while also trying to remove the last of the rope from her feet. She quickly stood and scanned the room for Jake. He was sliding his way toward the other side. Where was the pack? He must have lost it along the way. *Great*, she thought. *One gun, and it's between the devil and the disciple.*

Gail ran screaming toward Carlos, her arm raised in the air the entire way. To her the only way to save Taylor was to get rid of this evil man first. The two men seemed to freeze for an instant, and without taking his hand off the wrist of Liag, Carlos twisted his body around and, with his other hand, grabbed Gail's arm as it came down to stab Carlos in the back. Amanda heard the snap from where she stood. Gail shrieked as the knife dropped to the floor and her limp wrist bent at an unusual angle. With a crazed look in her eyes, Gail reached down for the knife before Carlos's fist came down hard on the back of her head. She slid to the ground unconscious.

Amanda moved toward Jake. He looked over at her and shook his head, lifted his hand off his wounded leg, and, with blood-soaked fingers, signed the letters *ELT* with his left hand. Amanda was confused for a second. *ELT*, she thought. *Ah, yes, the emergency locator transmitter.* There had to be one in the helicopter sitting outside the building. For a split second she wondered if she should take a chance and leave Jake. She knew it was a long shot, but Jake was right. The signal had to be sent if they hoped to get help anytime soon. Jake felt a sense of relief as he watched Amanda scramble unnoticed out the door. The sun was setting, and if they planned on using the helicopter to get out, it would be helpful to have at least the setting sun to help him see. Now if he could only get to his Glock. He hoped the piece had not been damaged. He dragged his leg behind him as he watched the two men carefully. As he inched closer to the wall, and the gun, he could see that Carlos had hold of Liag's right wrist, and Liag had hold of a gun. It was hard to make out the type, but Jake could see that the gun was pointed in his general direction as the two men fought.

CHAPTER 65

THE STRENGTH OF CARLOS WAS DEFINITELY STARTING TO WIN OUT OVER THE WILL OF LIAG. Jake was slowly moving toward his Glock, and Liag felt like he was starting to lose control of the situation. He couldn't understand how it had gotten to this point. He had planned everything out so well. He thought it would work out exactly as he envisioned it. "Carlos, listen to me. Have I led you astray? This is not the right time. You will not be welcomed into the spiritual world this way." Liag was perspiring with his efforts to control the large man, and he blinked as beads of sweat streamed into his eyes.

"No, I do not believe you. You are weak. You have brought me all this way. You had me build this ceremonial place of worship. You had me convince this girl of the rites and rituals so that we could bring her here. It has all come to pass just as we had said, and now you are trying to take all that we have worked for away from me. I will not allow it. You are just like everyone else."

Liag could see the rage in Carlos's face and knew what he needed to do. "Yes, OK, you are correct, Carlos. I was losing faith in your ability and I should not have. Let go of my arm and we can continue the ceremony." Liag looked skyward and Carlos followed his eyes. "Carlos, please, we are losing the light. The sun will be setting within the hour. If we are to continue, it must be completed now."

Carlos hesitated, then slowly released his grip on Liag. Jake rolled toward his Glock. Liag lifted his hand and aimed his gun directly at Carlos, who in one swift motion swung his sword from his side in a sweeping arc toward Liag's neck. Liag fired but not before Carlos was able to connect.

Jake got to his gun just in time to see Liag's body separate from the hood. The covered head flew off sideways, coming to rest on the altar at the feet of a now hysterical Taylor.

CHAPTER 66

AMANDA CHECKED THE AREA AND QUICKLY RAN TOWARD THE HELI-COPTER. She was nearly there when she suddenly felt a presence, a shadow from behind. Just as she dropped to the ground and rolled, an assailant flew over her, missing her by mere inches. She got up quickly and saw the guard jumping to his feet, looking for his gun, which had fallen off his shoulder about four feet from where he stood. Amanda dove into the brush directly behind her and ran as fast as she could, circling back behind the oval building to where the alcove was. She saw a hooded figure lying on the ground and knew Jake had been there. She heard the guard behind her running noisily through the brush. She had no time to think as a stream of bullets from his M16 passed by the left side of her head. She could tell the guard was near, and she ran as fast as her legs could take her. Feeling the adverse effects of her fever and infected arm, she dove over the body just as a second stream of bullets passed by. Amanda was partly under the body of the guard on the ground as yet another spray of bullets came her way. At first she thought she had been hit, but then she realized the blood was from the body next to her. *Well, if he wasn't dead before*, she thought, *he definitely is now.* The guard started to jog toward her, but his gun got caught in some brush, yanking the shoulder strap off. Huddled against the body for cover, Amanda felt something cold and hard. She reached into the folds of his robe and felt a gun. She slowly pulled out the Beretta. *Nice*, she thought. It would do the trick. She kept herself flat on her back, hoping the guard would think he had gotten her. Amanda concentrated. *Ten feet, eight feet.* She used nothing but her senses to tell her exactly where the guard was. *Five feet. OK*, she said to herself. *NOW!*

Amanda swung her arm out from behind the body and fired. The guard looked down at the neat bullet hole right where his heart was. As though time stood still for a moment, he could see the blood trickle down his robe as the pumping of his heart stopped just before he dropped like a marionette whose strings had just been cut.

Amanda hoped that was the last of the armed perimeter guards and moved quickly back in the direction of the helicopter.

CHAPTER 67

J.R. TOOK A SWEEPING TURN IN THE HELICOPTER AND DETECTIVE TAO'S STOMACH DID A BIT OF A SPIN. He had just realized that he had not eaten anything at all since lunch. He had given J.R. the last known coordinates of the Bannon party and hoped that somehow they would be able to connect. Tao knew they had got off to a late start, but he had filled out the paperwork as quickly as possible. The sun was starting to go down, but it was a cloudless day and there was still ample light to fly by. It didn't matter much, though, because J.R. was rated to fly at night and the helicopter was well equipped for search and rescue. He only hoped there was someone to rescue.

They circled the area where the Bannons had supposedly found a path into the jungle but couldn't see anything. "OK, Detective, we've circled this area long enough. I don't think we are going to find anything to help us here. We need to move in farther. How would you like to proceed?"

"Let's head north and see if there is any indication of activity." J.R. nodded and Tao pulled out his binoculars. They also turned on the infrared camera, which picked up the thermal heat from images. It was good enough quality to be able to tell a human from an animal.

They had been proceeding inward for about thirty minutes when the radio squawked, "Base to Phoenix One. Do you copy?"

J.R. pressed the transmit button on the mouthpiece. "This is Phoenix. Go ahead."

"Yeah, we just received word from the coast guard of an ELT transmitting about five miles east of your intended location."

J.R.'s eyebrows went up. "Base, registered ELT or unregistered?"

"Unregistered but digital GPS," came the answer.

"OK, where exactly?" J.R. looked excited, and Detective Tao had a fresh sense of hope. J.R. jotted down the information on the notepad strapped to his leg while Tao watched. He was always amazed at the coordination of helicopter pilots. It seemed as though they really needed three or four arms to fly the thing.

J.R. finished scribbling and then turned to the detective. "This should be them, Ron. It's an unregistered ELT emitting from the interior." J.R. could see Ron didn't understand, so he explained further: "An emergency locator transmitter in an aircraft can be registered or unregistered. If registered, which is the recommendation, they will have all kinds of information, like the type of aircraft, phone numbers, owner's name, etc. This one is not. However, we're lucky it's a digital model with GPS, so we can track their location to within three feet."

Tao was relieved, but he wondered who switched on the locator, the good guys or the bad.

"How did we get the information?" Tao asked.

Being an ex-military pilot, J.R. had a good working knowledge of how these things happened. "The U.S. government has about a $5 billion budget that goes to the NOAA, which is the National Oceanic and Atmospheric Administration, which, among many other things, has a subdivision called the NESDIS, the National Environmental Satellite, Data, and Information Service. These guys employ hundreds of people to watch and report on satellite information. They have standing rules on how to handle these types of emergencies. They don't act immediately, as it may be an accidental trigger or a test, but if the signal continues, they call it in."

"How long would it have to be going off before they called it in?" Tao wondered if they were too late.

"Because it is an unregistered signal, they would wait for a pass and call it on a second satellite. It could take up to six hours at the most." Tao's eyebrows furrowed. Six hours likely meant no survivors. J.R. caught his worried look out of the corner of his eye. "But not to worry, Ron. I got you covered. I called in a favor with my buddy who works with NESDIS. They were waiting specifically for any signal from this area. In this case, the signal is less than a minute old." Tao smiled. Good old J.R. He had been through enough strategic rescue missions to understand the importance of covering all possible options and leaving no stone unturned. This might be a successful SAR mission after all.

CHAPTER 68

AMANDA HAD JUST SWITCHED ON THE ELT WHEN SHE HEARD A GUN DISCHARGE. Then there was a high-pitched shriek. After a few seconds she heard another gunshot. *Oh shit*, she thought, her mind reeling at all the possibilities. She ran toward the building with the borrowed Beretta held tightly at her side.

Liag's shot had just missed, and as Carlos's sword came back down to his side, Jake had a clear shot and fired at the hulking man. Carlos stumbled backward and tripped. He slammed his head into the edge of one of the wooden tables as his body hit the floor. Flowers and candles fell to the floor around him.

Amanda ripped into the room just in time to see Carlos hitting the ground. She stuffed the gun into her pants and ran to the altar, where Gail's body lay. Amanda found the knife and cut Taylor free. That's when she realized the high-pitched sound had come from Taylor, whose mouth was frozen open as she stared in shock at the decapitated head sitting on the altar at her feet.

Amanda didn't have to look to know. Taylor was staring at the head of her father, Bernie Wright.

CHAPTER 69

GAIL WAS COMING AROUND. Amanda bent down and slowly lifted her head. "Are you OK to move?" she asked. Amanda wanted to get out of there as soon as possible and particularly didn't want Gail to see the head at the end of the altar.

Gail slowly raised herself up with the help of Amanda. When she finally realized Taylor was shrieking, she ran to her, cradling her in her arms, and then gazed down to the end of the altar. Gail's eyes widened and her mouth froze in a silent scream. Amanda walked up to her and slapped her hard across the face.

"We have to get out of here now, Gail."

"But . . . but . . . how?" Gail tried to form words, but only gibberish was coming out. "I can tell you what I know once we get out of this place. Come on!" Amanda left no room for argument. She yanked at Gail, who then half lifted, half dragged Taylor off the altar. Taylor had stopped screaming, but she was sobbing quietly into her mom's chest. They moved slowly toward the exit. Amanda rushed over and put Jake's arm across the back of her shoulders and moved herself into the crook of his arm, supporting his body and trying to take the pressure off his left leg. She had forgotten about her infected arm and her fever. Nothing else mattered right then other than getting into that helicopter. How well Jake could fly the bird with the limited use of his left leg she wasn't sure. But they had absolutely no other choice; they had to get help.

The four looked like something out of a war movie, heading frantically toward the helicopter, straggling along, leaving a trail of blood behind them, with Jake and Amanda hoping the ELT signal had gotten somebody's attention.

CHAPTER 70

"How long until we get there?" Tao asked. He was starting to get a very bad feeling as they moved deeper into the jungle.

"Oh, five miles in this baby will only be a few minutes, Detective. I imagine from the coordinates they should be somewhere just over that ridge there." J.R. pointed directly in front of them. "We'll do a flyover and get a better look before we put her down."

Tao nodded but wondered if a flyover was a good idea or if they even had the time. As they reached the edge of the ridge, which immediately flattened out, they could just make out a circular clearing in the middle of the brush. Tao couldn't believe the setup. There were a few bunker-style huts and a larger oval-shaped building in the middle, with a large opening in the center of the roof. Just as Tao was wondering if there were any signs of life, J.R. exclaimed, "There!" He pointed to the screen, which was linked to the infrared camera on the aircraft. Tao could see what looked like four figures coming out of the entrance of the building, but they were jammed together in pairs like they were stuck to each other. The sun was low and it was difficult to make out anything on the ground.

As they were passing over the main building, J.R. burst out, "There's one more inside the building." The camera picked up a large figure slowly moving through the open line of sight that the hole in the roof gave, then it disappeared once it was no longer in that clear area of the oval building.

Whoever it is, thought Tao, *he is quite a bit larger than the rest of them.* The figure seemed to be slowly making his way toward the exit, in the direction of the other four people.

CHAPTER 71

AMANDA DIDN'T NOTICE IT AT FIRST BECAUSE SHE THOUGHT the thump-thump-thumping was her pounding head from the fever that was now threatening to render her unconscious. She just wanted to curl up somewhere and fall asleep. But it was Jake who exclaimed, "Amanda, you did it! They found us!"

The sun was down, but in its afterglow Amanda could make out the shape of the Hughes NOTAR coming over the ridge and felt a sense of relief. At the same time, she had a tingling sensation as the hair on the back of her neck stood straight up.

They had reached the Bell, and Amanda helped Jake into the pilot's seat. "How fast can you start this thing up and get us out of here?" Jake started flipping switches without asking why, only hearing the fear in Amanda's voice. "I can get us up in two to three minutes."

Gail had scrambled into the back with Taylor wrapped tightly around her, and Amanda was just moving around to the passenger door when a giant figure in the darkness came swaying out of the building, holding the sword above his snake-tattooed head and moving directly toward them.

"What the hell is that?" J.R. said as he panned over and around the building. He had the spotlight on and the figure froze for a second to look up at the Hughes. "Looks like some kind of monk, but I don't think he's here to bless anyone with that giant sword he's brandishing. What should we do, Ron? It looks like the others are trying to get that JetRanger up."

J.R. was holding the helicopter in a hovering position. The detective took out his gun. "I don't think I'm going to be able to get a good shot at him, J.R." The evening breeze had picked up, and although the detective was a good shot, getting in close enough was too difficult. "I think we are going to have to land this puppy and give these people a hand. Just drop me off and keep her going in case you have to carry the rest of them. Radio in for help and I can catch a ride back with one of the other guys."

"Are you sure? What if there're more of them in the buildings and we can't catch them on the infrared?"

"I'll take my chances, but if two women and a girl made it out, I can. I am sure that if there were others they would have been out by now."

"OK." J.R. was skeptical but maneuvered the Hughes back over the building to a clear spot close enough for the detective to jump to the ground. Ducking away from the helicopter, he ran over to take cover against the wall of the oval building. Then he started to inch his way around, knowing he would eventually run right into the man with the sword. As he moved along he thought about that line from the movie *The Untouchables,* "Don't bring a knife to a gunfight," but for some reason that didn't seem to make him feel any better.

CHAPTER 72

AMANDA DIDN'T HAVE TIME TO THINK ABOUT WHO WAS IN THE
OTHER HELICOPTER OR WHAT THE HECK THEY WERE DOING. They
had moved away and she didn't care. She only cared about how quickly Jake
could get the JetRanger up.

Taylor screamed and pointed from the back of the helicopter, and
Amanda looked up in time to see Carlos in a full run toward them, blood
streaming from his upper right shoulder where Jake had managed to hit
him. The other helicopter had bought them thirty seconds while Carlos had
stopped to consider what it was doing. Then, as the Hughes moved away and
over the building, he saw that he only had one opportunity to finish the job.

"Fuck, fuck, fuck," Jake blurted as his fingers moved with lightning
speed and the blades started spinning faster and faster. Carlos was only ten
feet in front of them when Jake was able to pull slowly off the ground. The
winds were picking up, and it was difficult as the Bell was situated the wrong
way. Amanda looked up just as Carlos slammed the large sword down on the
front of the bubble window, cracking it. The loud crash made Amanda jump.
He then ran to the other side of the helicopter. They were now about five
feet up, and Carlos grabbed onto the helicopter's right skid, and Jake fought
against the weight.

"Can you manage it?" Amanda's voice seemed small amid all that was
going on. "This guy must weigh about 250 pounds, but she can take it," Jake

shouted back. He moved the helicopter forward, dragging Carlos's feet along the ground, hoping he could rub him off. Jake's left leg was bleeding horribly, and Amanda ripped off part of her shirt and tried to tie it around Jake's leg while he was moving the helicopter back and forth trying to shake Carlos off.

"Amanda! Not now! You're gonna have to get him off," Jake said sternly. "Give your gun to Gail. She'll have the best angle." Amanda immediately readied her gun and handed it to Gail in the backseat.

"Gail, you have to shoot him. You have the best chance of hitting him. I can't do it from here," Amanda said. Gail's hand trembled as she took the Beretta from Amanda.

They had climbed about thirty feet into the air, and Carlos was hanging straight down from the skids. Detective Tao had made it to the spot where Carlos had emerged from the building just in time to see the big man hanging from the skids of the Bell. Jake was doing his best to shake him off, and at that point Tao might have been able to hit Carlos, but he didn't want to take the chance of missing and hitting the gas tank as the Bell turned this way and that. He watched helplessly from the ground as it went higher and higher.

Amanda caught a glimpse of the man on the ground when she handed the gun to Gail. It was Detective Tao. She would have never guessed he would risk his job by coming for them. *Perhaps he has a soul after all*, she thought.

Gail slid open the back window of the Bell. She could get her arm through and a bit of her head to peek down and see Carlos. She was trying to angle herself the best she could to get a shot off. She pulled the trigger and missed. The bullet skipped off the right skid. "Gail," Amanda said, trying to steady her voice, "there are only three bullets left. You have to hit him." Gail nodded, but as she turned back to take aim, Carlos lifted his chin up to the skid, and she couldn't get a fix on him. He then swung his leg over the skid, and she realized this too late and screamed as Carlos caught her wrist and twisted the gun from her hand. He was now crouched on the skid and aiming the gun directly at the pilot's window and Jake.

Jake jerked the Bell to one side. Carlos slid around the skid while still managing to hold on to the gun. Jake spun the helicopter quickly in circles, then back and forth like crazy.

Carlos fell back to a hanging position with one hand gripping the skid and the other holding the pistol.

"I have to do something," J.R. said to himself. He had been hovering in the Hughes about two hundred feet away. He knew the pilot was pretty darn good at handling the Bell, but he could tell the big man wasn't going to give up until they were all dead.

The Bell was about three hundred feet in the air, and once he was clear of the trees and jungle, the pilot could pick up speed, J.R. was sure, and shake the man off. J.R. wondered if he'd have time. J.R. then flew the Hughes under the Bell. Jake could see the Hughes beneath him. "What the hell is this guy doing?" he said. Jake could see Carlos was trying to pull himself up again, but he stopped jerking around when he noticed the Hughes directly below him. Carlos took a shot at the Hughes and the bullet skipped off the rotary blade. It was nearly dark now and dangerous for two helicopters to be so close together. Jake was still trying to figure out what the other pilot was doing when he came up under them so close that Jake was sure they were going to collide and go down in a flaming heap of wreckage.

As Jake was about to spin away from the Hughes there was a spray of red and a sudden lift in the weight of the Bell. He looked down to see Carlos falling into the rotary blades of the Hughes. Jake immediately pulled up and to the left as fast as he could. Looking back, he watched as Carlos's mangled body rendered the rotary useless and the Hughes spun uncontrollably down into the jungle below them.

Detective Tao shook his head as the Hughes whirled chaotically out of control and crashed with a giant fiery explosion.

CHAPTER 73

AMANDA WATCHED THE CHILDREN RUNNING ALONG THE PATH AS SHE SAT ON THE SAND AT LAGOON TWO IN KO OLINA. Their mothers were yelling at them to stop running, but they continued on without a care in the world.

It had been about six months since the rescue of Gail and Taylor on the Big Island. She and Jake had decided to take a few months to see their kids in Canada and then do a European tour before coming back to Hawaii. Amanda needed to get away after their close call. Jake still walked with a bit of a limp, but he was diligent with his physio and you could hardly see the scar where the bullet went through his leg.

Amanda, on the other hand, had a long ugly scar from the cut on her arm as it had been infected badly and the skin didn't recover well from the wound.

Taylor had been placed in psychiatric care, and Amanda remembered the sad, lost look on her face when they finally landed safely at the Hilo airport, with emergency vehicles all around and authorities asking questions. Jake had flown back to pick up Detective Tao after the Hughes went down, so the detective had taken over all questions once they landed.

The weeks following the rescue were a blur. Between Detective Tao and Amanda, they were able to put the pieces of the puzzle together. *Such a sad story*, she thought. Bernie thought he had the ultimate plan. He had planned to eliminate Keith and blame Carlos, the fugitive, for the whole thing. He didn't realize how serious Carlos was about his beliefs. Bernie had planned to kill Carlos and escape, knowing that Amanda and Jake would get Taylor and Gail out. He would then be there for his family when they returned after experiencing this horrific event. He didn't think Amanda's insight was strong enough to see through his disguise, and it nearly worked except that his fake name, *Liag*, gave it away in the end. Even if he had escaped, Tao and Amanda had already figured it out.

Her cell phone interrupted her thoughts. "Hello, Detective, I was just thinking about you," she said into the phone as she smirked.

"Oh, your powers are beyond belief, Amanda," he said. She could imagine the smile on his face. They had become good friends, and Amanda asked about his family. "We're headed to Disney. Well, sort of . . . ," he trailed off.

"Oh, you're coming over to Oahu and the Disney Resort? Fantastic! It's right next door. Your son will love it!"

"Yes, I can't get the time off, but I think I will retire in a couple of years, and then I can take him to the mainland. In the meantime, I was wondering if you and Jake would be up to meet for dinner while we are there."

"Sure, we'd love to!" Amanda said enthusiastically, and then she got that stirring sensation in her belly. "Just dinner?" her voice was tentative.

"Well, there is this case . . . ," His voice trailed off.

Amanda cut in, "Oh, no you don't. . . . Well, let's talk about it over a nice glass of Saint-Émilion, and you're buying, Detective."

"My pleasure." Then he clicked off.

"I can feel you," Amanda said out loud.

Jake froze in the sand behind her. "Can't I ever surprise you?" He bent down and kissed the top of her head.

"Of course you can, and you always do!" She grinned and her eyes lit up as he handed her a beautiful rose and a strong Mai Tai.

About the Author

Desirée A. Bombenon, born in Colombo, Sri Lanka, is a successful CEO and certified strategic leader. She is a member of Young Presidents' Organization and has won several industry and leadership awards globally.

After twenty years of leading businesses, Desirée started her own wine importing and consulting companies. Balanced by her husband, Marc, and two children, Janine and Joel, Desirée travels extensively for business and pleasure. She volunteers for several community and philanthropic projects and serves on both business and non-profit boards.